JURASSIC SEA

A PREHISTORIC THRILLER

VIKTOR ZARKOV

SEVERED PRESS
HOBART TASMANIA

JURASSIC SEA

Copyright © 2016 by Severed Press

WWW.SEVEREDPRESS.COM

ISBN: 978-1-925493-29-0

ONE

Colt McKinnon had come out of the most terrifying few days of his life and seemingly landed in the lap of fame just a few weeks later. The day or so he had spent on what the media was now calling Jurassic Island (but what had been called Spectre Island by those in the know long before that) seemed like a distant nightmare now. At first, he had actually suffered nightmares where monstrous prehistoric beasts had devoured him...but those days were long gone. His terror had inexplicably morphed into the realization of just about every dream he'd had since the age of thirteen or so.

He'd been on countless new programs and talk shows. He'd been the featured speaker at countless seminars and he had even graced the cover of several magazines. He was getting calls from every network possible, some offering him obscene amounts of money to do nothing more than participating in lame reality shows. He'd also gotten a few offers from the larger networks, offering even more money to host shows about the supernatural, the unexplained and everything in between.

The day he was able to turn down a seventy-million-dollar contract for eight months of work, Colt knew without a doubt that his life had drastically changed.

But even rejecting that lucrative contract was nothing more than a distant memory now. Currently, Colt found himself standing at a small coffee kiosk in the offices of National Geographic. He'd just been interviewed for a special that would air next week. It was a two-hour interview that had been more draining than he had expected. But he thought it was going to be *the* interview to do more than just put him on the map (not that he wasn't already there). This was going to be the interview that solidified his place in history—the one that would finally get him the respect that he had been looking for ever since he stepped in front of a camera for the very first time and hunted for Bigfoot in the forests of Oregon.

He'd gotten congratulatory pats on the back after the interview. It had ended twenty minutes ago; all the lights had been dimmed, and the audio and video crews had gone their separate ways. There was a vibe in the air, the sort of buzz that came with a job well done. He had knocked the interview out of the park. He knew it, the network knew it, and even the very space within the building knew it. This was the first moment he'd had to be by himself, chugging down a cup of lukewarm coffee in the break room of a building he had coveted for a very long time.

As he drank it, he felt a slight vibration in his pocket. He almost ignored it; his phone had been blowing up ever since he'd gotten back to the States following the events on Spectre Island. But instinct was a hard thing to kill, so he pulled the phone out anyway. Secretly, he was still waiting on a call from someone in Hollywood to offer him a cameo in a horror movie.

So far, that had not happened.

When he saw the name on the display, he was glad he had decided to answer it anyway.

"Hey," he said, doing his best not to sound as tired as he felt.

"Are you done?" came a now-familiar female voice.

"Yes. We wrapped up about twenty minutes ago. How are you? This is an unexpected surprise."

"I know," the woman on the other end said. "We wrapped things up much earlier than expected. When I got back home, I found an interesting e-mail. And we can talk about what it entails when I see you again."

"And when might that be?"

The woman laughed seductively. "I've already a sent a car for you. It's probably already in front of the building. I figure it will take you fifteen minutes to get to my apartment. So…eighteen minutes, I guess."

"I'll see you then," Colt said.

He pocketed the phone and finished his coffee before hurrying out of the break room and down the hall towards the elevator.

The woman on the other end of the phone had been Nyoko Hisakawa. She was technically his employer and had been ever since the day her crew had rescued him off of Spectre Island. She had been the longtime nemesis of Joseph Thornton, the maniacal and rather self-obsessed man that had originally gotten him involved in the Spectre Island debacle (God rest his soul). Over a couple of weeks, the professional relationship between Colt and Nyoko had become something a little more and then had erupted into what Colt guessed could be considered a relationship of some sort.

Well, *relationship* might be a stretch. So far, there had been nothing more than a lot of sex and in-depth discussions about future treks that Nyoko would like for them to pursue. There were times when Colt wondered if Nyoko was only using the sex to keep him under her thumb. He was popular now and, whether she would admit it or not, was damn good at what he did. Honestly, if that *was* Nyoko's plan, Colt didn't mind. She had a ridiculously perfect body and never asked him for anything more than ample time in bed and discussions about subjects that Colt was passionate about. The woman was a genius in terms of technology, had a passion for the unexplained that rivalled his own, and seemed to be insatiable between the sheets.

All in all, it wasn't a bad situation to be in.

As Nyoko had said, there was indeed a car waiting for him outside of the National Geographic building. He got in and the car pulled off right away. To pass the time during the drive, Colt used his phone to flip through his e-mails and had one of those moments where he found it impossible to believe that this was the life he was living now.

In his inbox, he saw emails that read like a who's-who of pop culture and news. An interview request from someone at the SyFy Channel. An editor from *Rolling Stone* that was offering him the cover if he'd consider a ten-page interview space. A publishing house sending a fourth attempt to lure him into writing an account of what had happened on Spectre Island (their offer was now for fifteen million dollars with a two-million-dollar signing bonus).

And low and behold, finally…a casting agent wanting to know if he'd be interested in a cameo role in an upcoming horror movie.

Colt did a little fist pump in the back of the car. It was almost too much. He'd considered the book idea and was pretty sure he'd end up doing it. But not just yet. He'd have to wait until he was acclimated to this new lifestyle.

The car delivered him to the front of Nyoko's building less than twenty minutes later. When he stepped out of the car, he pocketed his phone and his thoughts turned instantly to Nyoko. When he thought of her in this way, there was nothing romantic about it. In fact, it made him feel like a lustful eighteen-year-old again. What they had was fun and a little dangerous, given that they worked together. And it was a very nice distraction from the whirlwind his life had become.

He took the elevator up to her large, four-bedroom apartment— the largest one in the building by far—and tried to do the math to his life. Had it really taken nearly getting devoured by prehistoric creatures to reach this amazing pinnacle? Something about that seemed deeply flawed, but he wasn't going to start complaining now.

He used his key to get into the apartment (Nyoko had given him one three weeks ago) and when he closed the door behind him, he started to get excited right away. He made his way through the living room, calling for her.

"Where are you?"

"Where do you think?" she asked, her voice both bossy and sexy at the same time.

He walked into the master bedroom and saw her lying on the bed in a sheer black thing that left very little to the imagination. Her flawless pale skin and black hair, let down over her delicate shoulders, seemed to call to him. It was every young boy's wet dream, like something straight out of a magazine.

"Um, I thought you said there was an e-mail," he said.

"There is," she said, propping her head up on her hand.

"What about?" he asked, toying with her.

"The Bermuda Triangle."

"A legit case?"

"I think so, yes. But...you really want to talk about that now?"

Sadly, a part of him did. But at the same time, the mostly naked lady on the bed was also equally important. But, like any man that had given in to the sight of a beautiful woman at least once before, it was a simple choice. The Bermuda Triangle had been there forever, and it wasn't going anywhere anytime soon.

But Nyoko's perfect naked body was here right now, three feet away from him, and it was his for the taking.

The Bermuda Triangle could wait. For now, there were other things to explore.

TWO

When they were done, they were both sweating and panting. Nyoko preferred long marathon sessions most of the time and Colt did everything he could to oblige. She was in perfect shape and usually recovered after a few minutes. Colt, on the other hand, was about twenty pounds overweight and only hit the gym once or twice a week and when he did, it was fleeting. He was still catching his breath when Nyoko walked into the adjoining bathroom and took a shower.

As he finally collected his breath, Nyoko called out to him over the sound of the shower water. "My personal e-mail is open on the laptop," she said. "There's an e-mail that's already opened for you. I think you might recognize the name of the sender."

Colt pulled his boxers back on and couldn't help but sneak a peek at her through the shower's glass door. Was this really his life? What did Nyoko see in him? Surely his assumption about her using sex just to keep him close was dead on. It's the only thing that made any real sense to him.

After all, she had been successful and incredibly wealthy before Spectre Island. She had inherited a tremendous fortune from her grandfather and was a powerhouse in the business world. Nyoko owned two Japanese television networks as well as one of Japan's largest telecom companies. Most of that had come from her grandfather, and she had built steadily upon it. The things she had gotten into and become successful at on her own included under the radar, cutting-edge scientific instrumentation. Her small yet ridiculously profitable tech company had millions tied up in the Large Hadron Collider project as well as a space tourism venture that the public didn't even know about.

And then, of course, she had her obsession with all things unexplained on the side. And that's why she had hired Colt after her team had rescued him from Spectre Island. They had discussed potential jobs since then, and he wondered if the e-mail he was about to read might be linked to it.

He pulled up the mail and his eyes grew wide when he saw the name in the sender field.

"Heath Francis?" he asked, a bit excited.

"Yeah, I know. Sorry I didn't tell you before now, but I wanted to make sure I had everything squared away."

"What are you squaring away?" he asked.

She didn't answer, so he read the mail. All it said was *Your plans sound good to me and I'm good to go. You know how to reach me if things change.*

"What's this about?" Colt asked.

The shower shut off and the door opened, revealing her naked form. Before Colt could sneak another peek, Nyoko had a towel wrapped around her.

"I've been getting some reports that there has been a spike in activity in the area known as the Bermuda Triangle over the past two weeks."

"Reports from where?"

"I have a few small floatation devices out in the area—updated versions of devices that my grandfather put out there years ago. And they've been feeding us some pretty interesting findings."

"Any disappearances yet?"

"No," Nyoko said. "All I've been able to come across are a few planes experiencing turbulence and temporary electrical failures. A single boat also reported rough waters that came out of nowhere, with no storm in sight."

"You'll have to excuse the ignorance of your non-science obsessed employee," Colt said with a smile, "but just what sort of use could readings from inside the Bermuda Triangle at a peak time do for you?"

"Tons," she said and got a sparkle in her eye that Colt had gotten used to. Nyoko loved to talk about work, especially when it came to the ins and outs of science. "I have a theory that magnetic shifts within that area will, on occasion, open dimensional rifts. This is based off of speculation that my grandfather wrote about. I believe that if I can catch the phenomenon in action, there's a chance that I could learn enough about it to apply it to scientific research towards space travel."

"That *is* sort of awesome," Colt said. Sometimes he felt like such a fanboy novice around her, and it made him feel very inferior.

"Yes it is," she said.

"And you kept all of this a secret from me?" he asked. "Weird stuff like this is sort of my thing, you know. The Heath Francis case is sort of legendary."

"I know. And that's why I didn't want to breathe a word of it to you until I knew for sure that it all checked out. That included getting Heath Francis in on it. I assume you know who he is?"

"Yes. He went missing in the Triangle for eight days in 2007. He was flying a small plane with five passengers, headed to Bermuda. Half an hour into the flight, all of his instrumentation went dead, and they flew into what Heath described as a bright white light. When they came out, they had somehow gotten turned around and were headed back to Florida. They had travelled about ninety miles in what they perceived to be less than ten minutes. When they landed, one of his passengers was in a coma. It was then, at the airport, that Heath and his passengers discovered that they had been missing for eight days."

"All correct," Nyoko said. "What you left out—and what never made it to the news, even to the seedier parts of the internet—was that one of his passengers committed suicide by hanging himself with a belt two weeks later."

"And how did you come to get in touch with Heath Francis?" Colt asked.

"He reached out to me about six months ago," she said. "Apparently, he went deep into the paranormal community and studied up on my grandfather. Heath said he keeps having dreams that seem prophetic. He says that if I ever wanted to understand the Triangle, he was pretty sure he knew the route to take me…well, *somewhere else.* He just thinks the time needs to be right."

"And you think that time is now?" Colt asked.

"I think the instrumentation we have out in those waters indicates that it's time for *something,* yes."

Colt thought about this and felt a stirring and familiar excitement within him. He'd been fascinated with the Bermuda Triangle for as long as he could remember. This was huge in terms of life ambition.

"His mail says he's *good to go,*" Colt said. "What does that mean?"

She smiled at him and placed her hand high up on his thigh, caressing him playfully. "It means we only have about an hour and a half before we have to meet him at the airport." She then leaned into him and whispered, "Any idea what we can do to fill the time?"

As they fell to the bed, he was ecstatic inside. Sex twice in a three-hour span with a beautiful woman and a trek into the Bermuda Triangle with a man that had been there and back.

Could life get any better?

THREE

Night had fallen by the time they reached the airport. They would be flying out of LaGuardia shortly before ten and arrive in Miami, after a brief layover in Atlanta, just after five o' clock in the morning. Colt typically hated to fly, but he planned on sleeping during the flights so he wouldn't be exhausted when they touched down in Miami.

To pass the two hours before their flight, Colt and Nyoko met Heath Francis in the airport bar. Colt found that he liked Heath right away. With several years of listening to people recount their paranormal experiences, Colt had a great bullshit detector built up. But it became quite clear to Colt that something strange had indeed happened to Heath…or at least he was convinced something had happened to him. The man's personality was also magnetic. He was in his early fifties, his hair going grey, and his face starting to show the first real signs of age. The man also told a story in a way that made Colt think that he night make a great grandfather someday, telling exaggerated bedtime stories to his grandkids.

Over mozzarella sticks, boneless wings, and several beers, Colt and Nyoko listened to Heath tell his story. Although they had both heard it before (Colt himself had read about it at least a dozen times and had seen Heath's brief appearances on several paranormal shows), they obliged him.

When he was done, Heath knocked out his third beer and looked longingly at the bar. He then averted his gaze to the table, as if he wasn't able to look at Colt or Nyoko for the last part of the story.

"There's something else," Heath said. "I've told Nyoko the briefest little bit about it, but not in great detail."

"What is it?" Colt asked.

"I remember absolutely nothing about those eight days we went missing. And I've called some of the passengers from the flight recently to see if they've maybe had some breakthroughs, but there's nothing. Still…I've been having these nightmares that honestly feel like premonitions. I know that sounds nuts, but it's the truth."

"What do you see in these dreams?" Colt asked. He noticed right away that Nyoko was sitting back in her chair, giving him an impressed grin. He knew that she enjoyed listening to him talk about the paranormal in the same way he enjoyed listening to her talk about science.

"It's just a bunch of images, really," Heath said. "Apocalyptic, horrifying images. I see a little plane flying through this white mist and there are these huge hulking shapes all around."

"Anything else?"

"No. That's it. And when I wake up, I'm fully aware that it was a dream, but at the same time, I also get the feeling that…"

"It's okay," Colt said, seeing the need in Heath to get it all out. He was a strong-willed man, that was evident, but he was also very expressive. In Colt's experience, that usually made for the best witnesses when it came to the unbelievable.

"I get the feeling that the things in the dream are a warning about the future but, at the same time, I'm supposed to be there. Does that make sense?"

"I understand what you're saying," Colt said, "but I'm not going to pretend that the need to be present for some terrible event makes sense."

Heath finally looked up and smiled. "You know, I knew who you were before all of the dinosaur stuff. I followed you pretty closely after my ordeal, actually. I'm really glad you're finally getting some attention."

"Yeah, I'm just not used to it. It's surreal. But I'm no different than any other paranormal enthusiast. At the risk of belittling what you've been through, I'm sort of stoked to be heading into the Triangle."

"For reasons I can't explain, so am I," Heath said.

"Maybe it's because men get off on putting themselves in harm's way," Nyoko joked.

"Possibly," Colt said. Heath and Colt had a laugh at this while Nyoko ordered another drink.

They passed their time like this until they heard the call for their plane on the overhead speakers. Nyoko bowed out first and paid the tab before the three of the walked to their gate together. There was a buzzing of excitement passing between them; even Nyoko, usually cool and calm in all situations, looked to be on edge.

They filed into the plane, the three of them managing to all sit together in a single row, as the flight was not crowded at all. As the plane waited its turn in line for take-off, Colt noticed how observant Heath was. He looked out of the window with great interest, eyeing the activity out on the runway. He also kept looking towards the front of the plane like a kid that was anxious to get a glimpse of the cockpit.

"Have you flown ever since what happened to you?" Colt asked.

"I went three years before I stepped foot on a plane," Heath said. "Just seeing a plane—small or large—terrified me. But I got over it and started small. I went to the small strip where I got my license and did some practice runs. After that, I was able to make a few small flights for clients, but nothing big."

"And as we discussed in our e-mails," Nyoko said, "there is a plane waiting for us at a small airport outside of Miami. I asked for a plane with your specifications—a Cessna 182, correct?"

"Yes, that's the one," Heath said. "I could fly one of those in my sleep."

"And you're fine to fly back out there?" Colt asked.

"Yes. I'm actually anxious to do it."

"Is there any way to guarantee that you can recreate the experience?" Nyoko asked.

"No. But I can take us to the exact spot and the exact height I was at when I disappeared in 2007. And if the area is as active as you say it is, that should be more than enough. I'll head straight towards Puerto Rico, as that last flight of mine was supposed to, and take the exact same course."

"And you feel certain you can handle any abnormalities that might present themselves?"

"I've read an exhaustive amount of material about the Triangle over the last seven or eight years," Heath said. "I know what to expect and am feeling pretty confident. And apparently, the worst that could happen is that we go missing for several days only to reappear mysteriously."

"I'm curious," Colt said, doing his best to shut down the idea of such a possibility. "Did you ever contact any other Triangle survivors in the years after you returned?"

"A few," Heath said. "None of them wanted to talk. I got the impression that they had all moved on and were trying to convince themselves that nothing had happened. Hell, I tried doing that myself. But with the dreams and the—well, the sense of invasion, I guess—I wasn't able to. I did the opposite. I became obsessed."

"Well," Colt said. "I relate to you there. It just so happens that I know a thing or two about being obsessed with the paranormal."

Heath gave Colt a shaky smile but looked back out of the window quickly. It almost seemed as if there was something out there that he did not trust—as if he was expecting something to reach out and snatch them right out of the sky at any moment.

FOUR

When they landed in Miami, the sky was still relatively dark. Dawn was about half an hour away as they claimed their few pieces of luggage and walked outside to find a cab that would take them to the small airstrip Nyoko had chosen. They filed into the cab, and Nyoko gave the driver the address to the airstrip.

Traffic let up once they got outside of the airport and they were able to watch the sun come up on the way. Colt found himself a little distracted, as he wanted to keep questioning Heath on the Triangle without seeming overbearing. It was also difficult for him to be around Nyoko due to the nature of their relationship over the last few months. To be in such a close proximity to her and knowing that they wouldn't be resorting to their normal amorous activities any-time soon was a bit disappointing.

"See that bruise-like color on the horizon?" Heath asked, almost out of nowhere. He was pointing to the right, at a rather beautiful play of colors from the rising sun. Colt saw the color he was indicating—a dark purple that was somehow one shade away from being both black and violet.

"What about it?" Nyoko asked.

"Just before the white lights took the plane, there was something in the air that, at first, I thought just an approaching storm. There were these thin clouds that were almost that exact same color. They gathered around the plane, almost like they were trying to pull the plane down, and then those white lights came.

There were also these thin pink strips in the air...I guess they were some form of light, too. Only, the pink ones seemed to be...alive."

"Alive how?" Colt asked.

The memory had apparently chilled him badly because all Heath did in response was give a shrug and look back out the window.

Colt and Nyoko remained quiet as Heath looked almost passively out of the window. For the first time, Colt felt slightly nervous about going up with Heath. What if they got several thousand feet in the air only to have Heath slip into some sort of post-partum fugue and put their lives in danger?

It's a little too late to be worrying about such things now, he thought himself. Besides, he had placed himself in many worse situations that this in the past and he had come out alive.

With the sun still nearing its rightful spot in the sky, the cab delivered them to a small airstrip that sat roughly ten miles outside of Miami's city limits. It was a small but well-cared-for facility with hardly any traffic and several small planes on their runways. When they stepped out of the cab, taking their luggage out of the trunk, Nyoko paid the driver, and they started directly for the office. Colt saw how quickly Nyoko was walking and had rarely seen her in such a rush. He assumed she was a bit on edge because the conditions within the Triangle could quite literally change at any moment.

After checking in with the office and getting the paperwork filled out, they were standing by the Cessna that Nyoko had reserved for Heath. While Colt placed their few bags into the plane, Nyoko stayed outside. She affixed two black devices to the bottom of the plane. They were nothing more than smooth black rectangles that equaled about eight inches across and three inches thick.

"What are these?" Heath asked, running his hand across one.

"These are synced to my laptop. They'll give me readings of the atmospheric conditions while we're inside the plane."

"What are we looking for, exactly?" Colt asked.

She smiled and said, "I don't quite know yet. But I'll know it when I see it. Magnetic shifts, for sure. Anything else…I just don't know yet. It's all based on the idea that magnetic fields can theoretically distort space and time. And magnetic fields also have the potential to create their own version of gravitational fields. You can feel those when you place two magnets close to one another. Then when you throw a thunderstorm into the mix, it ups the ante. It's an incredibly long shot, but there are also theories that conditions in a thunderstorm could alter gravitational and magnetic fields that are already screwy. Again, it's all shooting in the dark, but that could potentially be a recipe for space distortion."

"And now my head hurts," Colt said.

"Yeah, I don't follow all of that either," Heath said. "But trust me. You'll know when something is going to happen. I felt it in my teeth. Sounds weird, I know, but that's the first place I sensed some kind of a change. There's also a *weight* to everything, too. The whole plane just started to feel heavy."

"Splendid," Colt said. "Why don't we get out of here before I change my mind about this? And Heath…maybe we leave out the sight-seeing portion of the flight, okay?"

They all chuckled nervously at this as they climbed into the plane. Heath got adjusted behind the controls and checked the radio as Nyoko took the co-pilots seat, leaving Colt to sit alone behind them. Everything seemed to be in working order, and when they were given the go ahead to do so, Heath taxied out. As they headed down the runway, Colt stole a glance at Heath, looking for any signs that the man might be uneasy or even sacred about the trip they were about to take. Colt was surprised when he saw that Heath actually looked anxious—like an excited kid that had just got their driver's license and was sitting behind the wheel for the first time.

Still, Colt couldn't help but feel a slight queasiness as the plane left the ground and started its ascent. Sure, this was no different that flying in a plane with a pilot he didn't know sitting in the cockpit, but he *did* know that this certain pilot happened to have lived through a traumatic event while flying. That added a whole new level to things.

Once the plane was up and evening out, the land falling away beneath them, Colt could tell that Heath was relaxing a bit. His shoulders were drooped, and he seemed to soften back into the seat a bit.

"I won't lie about it," Heath said. "This feels pretty good."

"That's good to hear," Colt said, but his nerves were still a little chaotic.

With the plane levelling out and the flight starting on a smooth and positive note, Nyoko opened up her computer bag and powered up her laptop.

"I can't help but wonder," Heath said, nodding towards the laptop, "if that thing won't go all screwy on you. When it all went down for me, every single bit of instrumentation went down and we lost radio contact."

"I'm figuring that something like that will happen," Nyoko said. "I've got the software set to automatically save every ten seconds. That way if it all goes down, I have it backed up."

"Can I ask what you're hoping to find?"

"I don't know yet," Nyoko said. "But if the Triangle works the way folklore says it does, I believe there could be massive potential for learning how to perfect interstellar travel...or, at the very least, how to advance spaceflight."

Heath frowned at this and shrugged. "Space flight," he said. "Have you heard the Madison account within the Triangle?"

"No," Nyoko said.

"I've heard of it," Colt said. "But I don't know the specifics."

"Well, in 1988, this rich power couple, Don and Wendy Madison, were flying back to Florida from the Bahamas. They hit some turbulence in an area that is just right outside of the Triangle's center. According to their original testimonies, they started seeing these sparks of white light in the sky at the same time the turbulence started. The pilot tried changing course just enough to get them away from what they assumed was some weird heat lightning, but failed. The plane was consumed by the white lights.

"After that, the Madisons reported clear skies after just about ten seconds or so of the white lights surrounding the plane. But when they re-established radio contact, they discovered that the people on the ground weren't speaking English. In fact, they were damn near shot down."

"Why?" Colt asked. "What happened?"

"They came across the white lights about eighty-five miles north-west of the Bahamas and came out ten seconds later somewhere on restricted airspace over Russia."

"Are you serious?" Nyoko asked.

"Yes. The research is out there. And here's the kicker…for about a week, the Madisons screamed their story from the rooftops to anyone that would listen. It was all over the newspapers and television. They were extremely passionate about. But then they mysteriously started back-tracking. They totally changed their story, seemingly on a whim. Some think it was because of how they were treated in Russia when they landed. Others think it's because they were criticized and alienated from their elite rich friends."

"Is there any hard proof of this?" Nyoko asked.

"Leaked documents from a Russian Air Force base testify that a small-engine craft from America did indeed land on their runway on November 6th of 1988."

"That's crazy," Colt said. "Makes me wish I had spent more time looking into the Bermuda Triangle when I was on TV."

Nyoko looked back to him with a sly grin. "I'm pretty sure I'm paying you more than the networks were when you were on television."

"Touché," Colt said.

Heath carried them on, the bright morning flawless ahead of them. It was a perfect day, the sky crisp and clear and the landscape of sea beneath them calm and beautiful.

As far as Colt was concerned, it was almost too perfect. In his line of work, he knew better than anyone what the clam before the storm looked like.

FIVE

"How far away are we?" Nyoko asked.

They had been in the air for a little over an hour, and so far, they'd had smooth sailing. Still, Colt felt a building anticipation in his stomach. It was very much like being on a roller coaster and click-clacking up a large hill slowly, fully aware that there was a massive drop waiting on the other side.

Heath checked his instrumentation and looked out of the windows. The morning was still pristine, the sky bright and clear and the sea below like a perfect little miniature model of the world.

"I'm not positive," Heath said. "Twenty or thirty miles, maybe."

Nyoko looked over her readings on the laptop, her eyes rarely leaving the screen. "I don't see any shifts or changes here."

"I don't want to be the voice of dissent here," Heath said, "but I don't know that you *will* see any changes. Like I said before, I've read tons of material on the Triangle. You aren't the first person to try something like this—to capture readings from inside the area. There has been minuscule data here and there, but never anything substantial."

"I can appreciate that," Nyoko said, "but I doubt any of the people that have tried this in the past had equipment like mine."

"She's sort of a mad scientist in a way," Colt said. Nyoko turned and sneered at him. He shrugged lazily and smiled at her.

"You know," Colt added, "having been on a few trips where the unexplained was sort of the focal point, I know how unpredictable all of this can be. So shouldn't we have some sort of contingency plan just in case this doesn't work?"

"Meaning what?" Nyoko asked.

"What if we *do* get taken somewhere else, but it's not the same as what happened to Heath the first time? We have no idea what we're heading into. What if we get zipped back to the Civil War or way off into the future?"

"I guess we'll wing it," Nyoko said with a bit of dry humor in her voice.

"It looks like that might be all we have time for," Heath said. "Look up ahead."

Colt looked through the windshield and saw nothing at first. But then, just ahead of them, was a soft mist. He supposed it could be seen as the tail ends of clouds, only there were no clouds anywhere near them. He was pretty sure they weren't flying high enough to be weaving through clouds.

"That mist?" Nyoko asked.

"Yes."

"Did you see it before?"

"No. But a great deal of reports from Triangle survivors report a mist that is almost like sporadic light rain. It comes out of nowhere. If the stories ring true, we'll pass through that and then there will be a thunderstorm shortly after that.

No one spoke as Heath guided the plane towards and then through the mist. Colt almost remarked on how much darker the plane seemed to get as they passed through it. He looked out of the side window, peering down to the ocean. Nothing had changed down there, but inside of the plane, it looked and felt as if the sun had suddenly been covered by clouds. He didn't say anything about it because the looks on the faces of Heath and Nyoko made it clear that they had noticed this, too.

It took only a handful of seconds for Heath's prediction to reveal itself. The sound of thunder rumbled all around them. Colt felt the reverberations of it in his seat. Nyoko glanced back to him quickly with bewilderment in her eyes.

"And here are the storm clouds," Heath said, pointing ahead. There was now the smallest infliction of fear in his voice, and it spread through the plane like a virus.

Colt looked ahead and saw a series of dark clouds that had not been there twenty seconds earlier. It seemed as if the mist they had penetrated had been hiding them. They had literally come out of nowhere.

"Last chance to back out," Heath said. "I still have time to fly over or around them. Your call."

"Are you all in?" Nyoko asked.

"Yes," Heath said. "I'm ready to go."

"Colt?" she asked.

His need for exploring the unexplained won out, as always. "Yeah. Let's do it."

"You two are just as crazy as I am," Heath said.

They flew straight ahead, the clouds coming forward as if they were actually moving towards the plane. Colt looked ahead and saw something else within the folds of the storm clouds. It looked like flashes of heat lightning, white lines of energy knitted within the clouds. But he knew this was not heat lighting. These were the same white lights Heath had seen on his original trip.

"Look familiar?" Colt asked.

"Exactly like I remember it," Heath said.

Thunder continued to rumble, and the clouds grew thicker. Colt once again peered out of the window, looking down to the sea. He could barely see it now, as the clouds had grown so thick and tight to the plane that they blocked out most of the view.

"I'm getting some changes to these readings," Nyoko said. "The magnetic fields are…well, they're behaving oddly. These numbers don't make any sense and—"

Colt was looking over her shoulder as the laptop went to black. Nyoko hit the power button repeatedly, but got nothing.

"No use," Heath said. "I just lost everything, too."

Colt looked to the navigation instruments and saw that the needles were all waving back and forth, almost like a metronome. "So you still have engine power?" Colt asked.

"Yes. I can throttle and pull back, but the steering is gone. This happened last time. Whatever this thing is—a wormhole or tunnel or whatever you want to call it—it has us now, and it's doing the driving."

"What's that?" Nyoko asked. She pointed ahead to where the storm clouds started to take on a dirty yellow tint. Beyond that, the white lights were growing more prominent, and they appeared to be swirling.

The plane began to shake. A series of creaking noises filled the cabin. Up front, Nyoko let out a little yelp of shock.

"It wasn't this bad before," Heath said. He was fighting with the steering, still unable to get the plane to respond.

Thunder boomed around them as they neared the odd yellow-tinged clouds. The plane felt as if it had been pushed hard to the left. As they all recovered from the impact, Colt felt a peculiar sensation that was bother alarming and awe-inspiring. For a period of about five seconds, he felt weightless. He was aware that they were moving forward, the yellowish clouds now surrounding them, but he also felt stationary, almost like he was suspended in space. He opened his mouth to ask if Heath or Nyoko were feeling this, too, but he was unable to speak. There was a pressing weight within the plane that was uncomfortable but not to the point of being dangerous.

And then, just like that, the clouds were gone, and Colt felt himself settling down. The sense of weightlessness was gone and outside, the sky was bright once again.

"Did you guys feel that?" Colt asked.

"Sort of like floating," Heath said. "Yes."

"Did we come through, then?" Colt asked.

"Seems that way," Nyoko said, powering up her laptop again. This time, it came on but Colt only gave it the smallest bit of attention.

"We do have one very serious problem," Heath said. "I can steer again, and most of my nav tools are up and running, but something's not right. We're slowly going down, and I can't bring it back up. I can only decrease the angle of descent. Pretty sure one of the engines is shot."

"So we're going down?" Nyoko asked.

"Yeah. That's putting it lightly."

They all looked out of the windows, hoping for any sign of land. But all there was to all sides was the ocean. In the back of his mind, Colt wondered if it was the same ocean they had been flying over before passing through the mist, the thunderstorm, and the odd clouds.

As he looked out, the water drew closer and closer. The morning was back to being bright and blue again, but the approaching water suddenly looked very menacing.

SIX

As they continued their uncontrolled descent towards the sea, Nyoko was furiously typing commands into her laptop. Colt saw a map of the area that made up the Bermuda Triangle and a series of digital numbers along the bottom of it. He wasn't certain, but he was pretty sure she was trying to pinpoint their location. The frustration and fear on her face made Colt assume that it was not going well.

"Heath, how hard are going to hit?" Colt asked.

"Fortunately, it may not be so bad. It won't be a picnic, either, though. I estimate that we have about forty-five seconds before we hit. If you'll look in the back in that small closet, you'll find life preservers and, hopefully, an inflatable life raft."

Colt ran to the back, having to hunch over and fight for traction against the descent of the plane. He found the closet right away, in the far rear of the plane. When he opened it, several items fell out due to the plane's steady descent. There were several life preservers, a flare gun, rope and a small toolbox. In the back, an orange plastic-like bundle was tied down. Fairly certain that this was the life raft, Colt unhooked it from the wall and pulled it out.

He rushed back to the front and froze for a moment when he realized just how close they were to crashing into the sea. Nyoko has finally closed her laptop and was looking desperately back at Colt. He had never seen her so alarmed before, and it made him want to do everything within his power to protect her.

He handed her one of the life vests and then put on his own. As he clicked it closed, he looked out of the windshield. He could no longer see the sky; there was only the approaching sea. While it was coming up relatively slowly, he could still tell that the amount of speed they had to their descent was going to make this one hell of a crash.

He handed another of the life preservers to Heath, and he managed to get it on without surrendering full control of the plane.

"Sorry, guys," Heath said. "Colt, you might want to buckle up."

Colt ran back to his seat and grabbed the buckle. As he did, he chanced another look out of the windshield. In front of him, Nyoko screamed. With a moan of desperation rising up in his throat, Colt looked at the windshield just as he clicked his buckle. Heath had managed to pull the plane up just enough to prevent the nose of the plane from going into the water. Still, the plane was not level at all.

Colt was looking through the windshield when they hit. Water splashed up all around, and the plane shook violently. Colt felt the plane pitch forward, the seatbelt digging violently into him. Heath cried out and Colt watched the man's head snap back hard. The windshield cracked in several places and there was a splintering sound from outside.

Miraculously, it was over after that. There was only the sound of water and the aggravated ticking noises of the engine.

"Everyone okay?" Colt asked, still not quite believing that it was already over.

"Yeah," Heath said. "Just the worst whiplash in history."

"Unh," Nyoko said. She sounded like she was in pain.

Colt unbuckled and went to her side. She was bleeding from the mouth and holding her head. He looked her over for any visible injuries but saw nothing right away. "Are you okay?" he asked.

"I bumped my head on the side of the plane and bit my tongue," she said. "But I'm fine, other than that."

Behind Colt, Heath was trying the radio. It was working but only offered them static. Colt watched as Heath ran through the channels, only to get ambient noise and static as a response. In frustration, he slapped at it and gave up.

"We're on our own," he said.

"So what do we do?" Colt asked.

"I've never crashed before, so it's just as new to me as it is to you. But protocol says to radio for help. And since that idea is out of the window, I say we just get ready to hang out at sea for a while."

"Is that safe?" Nyoko asked.

"Should be. There's the life raft," he said, nodding to the package still held in Colt's arms.

"I saw a flare gun back there, too," Colt said.

"Good. That's the best we can ask for."

"How long before the plane sinks?" Nyoko asked.

"No clue. But when it starts, it'll go fast. So get whatever you think you'll need to survive and get ready to get on that raft."

Nyoko instantly started slipping her laptop into her bag, which had been thrown far under her seat in the crash. She spit blood onto the floor and grimaced.

"You sure you're okay?" Colt asked.

"Yes. I'm fine. You know how to work that raft?"

"I think so."

Heath was standing now, looking around the plane. All around them, it was creaking. And as Colt also took in the shape of it, he noticed the water seeping in along the left wall, low to the floor. It came in a steady stream, pooling on the floor and slowly making its way to the back.

"Might as well go ahead and get it set up," Heath said. "I can do it if you want. My plane, my disaster. I need to take care of my crew."

"It's okay," Colt said. "I can handle it. Why don't you try out the radio again?"

Heath shrugged but went back to the front anyway. He tried the radio, speaking into the mic and giving their status and location. Hearing him speak the words *"downed craft"* was chilling, so he stopped listening.

He walked to the middle of the plane where the door remained tightly closed. He reached out for the handle above the words EMERGENCY EXIT. "Is this safe?" he asked up front.

"Yes," Heath said. "Just stand back in the event that any water comes rushing in."

Colt stepped back a bit and then pushed down on the emergency handle. There was a bit of resistance when he pushed the door, but it finally opened. A small bit of water sloshed in over the side, but otherwise, he was in the clear. With the door pushed open, he looked outside and saw a never-ending expanse of the ocean.

"Any idea where we are?" he asked.

"No," Nyoko said, joining him by the opening. "I tried to pull it up on the GPS software just as we were going down. But it was unresponsive."

"And what did you think of those weird readings you were getting before we went down?"

"There were some definite magnetic shifts, that was for sure. The weirdest thing of all, though, was that readings for the weather and barometric pressure dropped to zero all across the board. When we were in those clouds, it's as if there was no weather at all to report. Not even a temperature."

"On that note," Heath said, sliding up next to them, "let's get out of this plane. It's taking on water slowly, but I'd rather get out now while we have the time rather than making a run for it as it goes down."

Colt nodded and, rather tentatively, held the cord of the deflated raft. He then reached out of the plane and dropped the raft into the water. He gave the cord a pull and the raft inflated quickly—so fast that he took a stumbling step back in surprise.

With the raft blown up just outside of the plane door, Heath motioned for Nyoko to climb on. "Ladies first," he said.

Nyoko held on to the side of the doorway and stumbled into the raft. She had her laptop bag over her shoulder, which seemed silly to Colt. She clung to it as she positioned herself safely in the raft.

"Go on," Heath said, patting Colt on the back. "I'll grab the flare gun and then I'm right behind you."

Colt steadied himself in the doorway and climbed over into the raft. He made his way over to Nyoko and then looked all around. He was hoping to see some signs of land, but there was only the sea. It made him feel small, helpless, and altogether inconsequential.

Seconds later, Heath appeared in the doorway. The raft had bobbed and floated slightly away from the door, so he had to jump into the raft, nearly falling into the water. Colt helped him slide into the raft and the three of them sat close together, looking out to the sea. In front of them, the plane bobbed uselessly in the water.

"So now what do we do?" Nyoko asked.

Heath unzipped a small compartment along the interior of his side of the raft. He pulled out a few items that Colt had not bene expecting to see in an emergency compartment of a life raft: a small flashlight, a folded canopy, and a collapsible paddle.

Heath removed the paddle and unfolded it. "We paddle until someone finds us," he said. "And if worse comes to worse, we'll shoot off a flare. But we need to wait on that; this early, this bright, a flare can easily go unseen."

"So we paddle…" Nyoko said.

"Yes," Heath said. And with that, he placed the paddle in the water and pushed away from the plane which, Colt was sad to see, had indeed started to slowly sink.

SEVEN

In the course of his career, Colt had been in some precarious situations, but he had never been stranded in the middle of the ocean. It wasn't scary per se, but it did paint a perfect picture of just how small he was. The waves were gentle and lazy, but they still carried enough power to bob their raft along. Heath had been rowing them ahead for the last twenty minute, and as his arm got tired, he handed the oar to Colt.

"You mind taking over?" he asked.

"Not at all," Colt said, taking the oar and setting to work. Honestly, he didn't really see the point in rowing, but he didn't think it was worth an argument. If they were going to be floating around in the ocean, why not just let the ocean carry them where it wanted? If a plane or boat was going to rescue them, the ocean would do just as good of a job pushing them to wherever it wanted than they could with a single oar.

He found, though, that the simple act of rowing kept his mind focused on something other than the dreary fact that he had just survived a plane crash into the ocean and that there was no land in sight. He glanced over to Nyoko and saw that she was looking out to the water with a blank expression on her face. There was dried blood on her lip, and her hair was disheveled. He had never seen her look so vulnerable, and it made him feel a little uneasy.

He looked back towards where the plane had crashed and could just barely see it glistening in the morning sun. It was nearly full submerged now, the entire back end in the water and the front pivoting upwards slightly.

As he watched, something popped up in the water directly in front of it. It was a hump-like shape that slithered almost casually, coming up and then under, still hidden, almost like all of the faked footage he had ever seen of the Lochness Monster.

"Look back at the plane," Colt said, the rowing forgotten for the moment. "I want to make sure I'm not the only one seeing that."

Heath and Nyoko looked back, and the gasp of surprise from Heath was enough to prove that Colt wasn't imagining things. Whatever it was that he had seen was still there, only now there was more of it. It had breached the water seemed to be studying the wrecked plane. The distance made it hard to make out any discernable features to the thing, but Colt was fairly certain he could rule out dolphin or shark.

The closest thing he could place beside the creature he was seeing was a swordfish, but the shape of this thing was off...not only in size but in the way it managed to sort of float up alongside the plane. As it came to the side of the plane, he got a better idea of the shape of the thing and it made even less sense.

"Either of you know what that is?" he asked.

"No clue," Heath said.

"I'm really trying not to jump to conclusions," Nyoko said.

Colt wasn't either. But from what he could tell, the thing that was currently exploring the surface of what had been their plane seemed to have a neck. More than that, it seemed to have a long neck. On top of that neck, an almost cone-shaped head prodded at the wreckage.

"Colt?"

It was Nyoko, apparently coming to the realization that they were indeed seeing this—they were looking at a *Cryptoclidus* swimming alongside the wreckage of the plane.

"Yeah?"

"Is it…?"

"It's impossible, but yeah. It looks like a *Cryptoclidus*."

"A what?" Heath asked.

"A *Cryptoclidus*," Colt said. "It was a kind of plesiosaur that is thought to have thrived during the Mid-Jurassic period."

"Jurassic?" Heath asked. "Like…dinosaurs?"

"Yeah."

Heath let out a nervous laugh. "How's that even possible?"

It started to fall in place for Colt, and a shudder passed through him. The words came to him, and when they did, they came out easily. For anyone else, the words might reek of lunacy. But he'd seen and done some things that most other people had not—things that made seeing a *Cryptoclidus* swimming in the ocean next to a wrecked plain not *strictly* impossible.

"I guess the tunnel or vortex or whatever the hell it was that we flew through took us back quite a ways."

"That's ridiculous," Heath said. "No way…"

"Hey, I feel the same way," Colt said, his eyes still on the creature. He stared out at the *Cryptoclidus* and shook his head, thinking: *What is it with me and dinosaurs as of late?*

EIGHT

They watched the *Cryptoclidus* poke around at the plane until it apparently got bored. It dove back underwater, its backside revealed above the water for a split second. Seeing its tail and the way it hit the water as it descended was the last bit of proof Colt needed. He was not a dinosaur expert—he had only ever really known just a bit more than the bare basics, and that had been due to research from when he'd been on television—but he was pretty damn sure that the thing they had just seen was a *Cryptoclidus*.

That opened up another question: if they had just seen a *Cryptoclidus* and they were floating in a Jurassic-era ocean, what other monsters lurked underneath them? It was a terrifying thought and, as such, Colt did everything he could to banish it from his mind.

As if reading his mind, Nyoko looked at him sternly. "So what does this mean?" she asked. "If we assume that your theory is correct, what do we do about it?"

"Hell if I know," Colt said. "I think the one hope we do have is that it's not just planes that go missing in the Bermuda Triangle; it's boats, too. And if that's the case, then I'd assume there's access to one of those cloud-tunnels somewhere on the water."

"So we keep rowing until we see those white lights or any sign of a thunderstorm?" Heath asked.

"That's the only thing I can think of," Colt said.

He continued to row, each thrust pushing him a minuscule distance forward. He glanced back to where he had seen what he thought had been a *Cryptoclidus* and saw that the plane was now gone. There were about two hundred yards between there and where they currently floated. The idea that there might be a *Cryptoclidus* swimming in the waters between the two spaces was a little terrifying and Colt wondered if dipping a paddle into the water and making even the smallest of commotions was the smartest thing.

"Look," he said. "If that thing is anywhere near here and not racing back down below, then sticking this oar in the water and splashing around is just about the worst thing we could do. We don't want to be attracting attention."

Nyoko removed any chance of an argument by reaching over and yanking the oar out of his hand. She tossed it into the raft and looked at both Colt and Heath as if they were crazy.

"Hold on," Colt said, doing his best to look her in the eyes. She met his gaze, but only for a moment.

"What?" she spat.

"We can't freak out right now," he said. "We have to keep our heads."

There was venom in the gaze she directed at him, but he didn't let it bother him. She looked back out to the water, and he felt sorry for her. He knew her well enough to know that she was already blaming this entire situation on herself. He would have loved to give her some encouraging words or, at the very least, tell her that it wasn't her fault. But he also knew her well enough to know that she'd only blow up on him and lose her patience with him if he tried consoling her. While their relationship was mainly only sexual in nature, he *had* gotten a few glimpses of her inner workings.

They floated in stunned silence for a moment, a quiet that was broken by a brief spurt of nervous laughter from Nyoko. "Get a load of this," she said.

"What?" Colt asked.

She held out her wrist, showing them her watch. It was an expensive model but had a read-out that resembled a cheap, old-school digital watch. Colt had observed it before and knew that it showed the Eastern Time in the US as well as the time in Tokyo. It also had a calendar of sorts along the bottom.

Now, however, the watch was nothing more than a series of digital shapes. A few of the little digital marks seemed to be flickering madly.

"Maybe it got wet?" Heath asked, although the tone in his voice indicated that he knew very well that this was not the case.

"This watch is water resistant to one hundred and twenty feet," she said.

"So it's the time discrepancy," Colt said. "Let's just call it what it is. Still...it makes no sense. If it's digital and run by a battery, why would it be affected?"

"I don't know," Nyoko said, looking at the watch as if she wanted to throw it into the ocean. She snapped her answer out, making it clear that she was still irritated.

Setting Nyoko's mood aside for the moment, Colt turned his attention to Heath. "So when we started going down, how far off course did we get from the location where you first entered the tunnel?"

"All of the navigational readings were down," he said. "So it's impossible to tell. But if I had to go off of pure instinct, I'd say not too far."

That's assuming that we only moved through time, and not space, too, Colt thought. Yet, even if they *had* been moved through space, he thought that whatever powers worked in the Triangle had their own highways and spaces. He didn't think the same rules of space applied when it came to wormholes and vortexes or whatever the hell they had just passed through.

"Why?" Heath asked. "What are you thinking?"

"I'm wondering if the time-slips in the Triangle work like a road," he said. "I wonder if there's a...well, a highway for lack of a better term...somewhere right around us and we don't even see it."

"And what if there is?" Nyoko asked. "So you suggest we just ride through it on this raft? You felt how rough it was on the plane!"

He wasn't about to get into an argument with her, so he let the issue lie. Instead, he looked back out to the ocean, in the direction of where the plane and the *Cryptoclidus* had been.

Fortunately, it seemed like Heath had his back.

"If it's the only plan we have, I say we go with it," Heath said. "After all, if we *have* slipped back to some prehistoric time, it's not like we're going to be rescued by a plane or boat, right?"

The irony of what happened next could not have been scripted better. When it happened, Colt actually let out a laugh—perhaps a laugh at their situation or at the overall absurdity of how the universe worked sometimes.

"What's funny?" Nyoko asked him.

Colt pointed at what he had seen behind them, hazy on the horizon. Heath and Nyoko turned, and when they saw it, too, Nyoko also laughed.

"Is that...a boat?" Heath asked.

"Looks like it," Colt said. "Maybe a ship of some kind. Hard to tell."

"Which way is it going?" Nyoko asked. "Can you guys tell?"

Colt looked out to the shape that was a little too close to the horizon for his liking. It was only a black, boat-shaped object for now. It was next to impossible to tell which way it was headed just yet.

"Sorry I yanked the oar away," Nyoko said, nudging it back to Colt.

"No problem," he said dismissively.

Colt started rowing in the direction of the boat, relieved to find that he now actually seemed to be rowing *with* the power of the ocean rather than against it. Still, it took him no time to realize that there was no way in hell that they were catching up to that boat. It also occurred to him that a boat in the middle of a prehistoric sea made just about as much sense as...well, as a crashed plane in a prehistoric sea. He could only assume that the boat was also a victim of the Bermuda Triangle.

"Look over there," Heath said, pointing to his right.

Colt looked and saw several humped shapes surfacing above the water a good distance away, though not quite as far away as the plane and the *Cryptoclidus* had been. Colt couldn't be certain, but he thought it might be the same creature. And if that were the case, it was getting closer to them. He did his best to make each stroke of the raft as minimal as possible, dipping the oar in carefully and then pushing forward slowly and delicately.

The three of them shared a look that seemed to translate a single message: *Be quiet. Don't do anything that would attract attention.*

Nyoko continued to hug her laptop case, almost like it was a secondary life preserver. Heath, meanwhile, kept an eye on those moving humps as they disappeared for a moment and then reappeared. From what Colt could tell, the thing wasn't coming *at* them but seemed to be swimming adjacent to them. If it *did* know that they were there, it looked to be almost playing with them.

Colt looked ahead and saw that they may have at least one lucky break playing in their favor. He was now fairly certain that the ship they had spotted was headed in their direction. It was a good distance to the left—in the opposite direction of the *Cryptoclidus*—and had gotten a bit larger in size rather than smaller and shrinking away.

The next fifteen minutes or so passed in that same way. The three of them would look from the area where the *Cryptoclidus* was sometimes partially breached and showing its humps, to the slowly approaching ship. As they got closer to it, Colt realized that the speed of the boat was odd. It looked to be coming quickly one moment and then stalled the next. It was obviously hard to be sure of anything about it due to the pitch and pull of the ocean, but there was certainly something *off* about the boat.

"What kind of boat is that, anyway?" Heath asked.

Colt had been wondering the same thing. It looked too small to be any sort of carrier ship and was too large to be a private vessel of any kind.

"Is it a cruise ship?" Nyoko whispered.

That had been Colt's next guess, but he didn't think that was quite right, either. It had the look of a luxury liner but it—

"Heath," he said, understanding finally dawning on him. "You said you're sort of a Bermuda Triangle expert now, right?"

"Yeah, I guess."

"Throw logic out the door for a minute and tell me something…is that the *Princess Celeste*?"

Heath was quiet for a moment but then let out a gasp of disbelief. "My God. What if it *is?*"

"What's the *Princess Celeste*?" Nyoko asked.

"A passenger ship that went missing in the Triangle in 1945," Colt said.

"One hundred and two people on board," Heath said. "And none of them were ever seen again."

"And you both think this might be that ship?" Nyoko asked.

Colt and Heath shared an uncomfortable look before Colt said, "There's only one way to find out."

NINE

It took another twenty minutes of tense moments, but the ship finally came close enough so that they could see proof of Heath and Colt's speculations. Printed along the side of the ship, right at the front in faded white letters, were the words: *The Princess Celeste.*

"This is unbelievable," Colt said.

Beside him, Nyoko dug into one of the smaller pockets of her laptop bag and retrieved her cell phone. She opened the camera and started snapping a series of pictures. Colt watched her, but only fleetingly. His attention was focused more on the massive humps in the water that was still keeping track with them. The *Cryptoclidus* was still keeping its distance, but for the thing to have actually followed them so far, it *had* to be aware of them. It was almost as if it were escorting them through the strange waters.

"How do we get on?" Heath asked, his eyes locked on the ship.

The ship was coming up slowly, and it was then that Colt understood that the boat was simply floating lackadaisical in the ocean. There were no engines running; the thing was just bouncing along in the water.

"There," Nyoko said, pointing to the rear of the boat. Colt followed her finger and saw a dingy old ladder along the back. It clung closely to the boat's body, and he assumed it was some sort of ladder to be used or for emergencies when the boat was docked. It looked to climb the entire back of the boat, coming to an end on an indented level just above the main floor.

"Let me see the oar," Heath said, offering his hand.

Colt gladly gave it over, his shoulder beyond sore from the half an hour or so of rowing. As he did, he glanced back to the *Cryptoclidus* and saw that it seemed to be closer. And, unlike the Princess Celeste, it was also moving. In fact, it seemed to be angling closer to them. He was pretty sure the *Cryptoclidus* only ate bottom-dwelling creatures like shellfish, but he didn't feel like testing the waters to see if it had any desire to try human flesh.

"Angling up right to the back of the boat is going to be a bitch," Heath said. "Colt, can you get to the very edge of the raft and do everything you can to grab hold of that ladder?

Colt went to the opposite side of the raft and looked to the boat. There was about twenty feet between them now and at the rate they were going, given the angle and the slow rate of speed the raft was capable of, he was afraid that they would bounce right into the damn thing and go careening further away from it—directly in the direction of the *Cryptoclidus*, in fact.

"Nyoko," Heath said. "I need some more oomph on this oar. Come help, would you?"

Awkwardly, she strapped her laptop bag over her shoulder and stumbled over to the side where Heath was rowing from. He adjusted his grip, taking the top portion of the oar and gave Nyoko the lower half. It looked silly, and it took them a while to get in sync, but when they got it working, Colt noticed a drastic difference in the way the raft moved. Apparently, Heath knew what he was doing; the raft was still going to come very close to striking the side of the boat rather than sneaking in behind it, but their chances were much better than they had been two minutes ago.

Colt couldn't believe that he was about to attempt to board the *Princess Celeste*. This boat was the thing of legends, the topic of more than a dozen ghost stories concerning the sea and—

A sudden motion to his right caught his attention. He looked over and saw that the *Cryptoclidus* had come much closer. It was so close now that he could see the water glinting off of its hide in the sunlight. No more than thirty feet separated it and their raft, giving Colt a much better estimate of its size. The thing was fifty feet long *at least*...and that was an estimate based solely on the thing's humps.

It drew closer and closer as the boat neared. For every few feet they got closer to the boat, the *Cryptoclidus* seem to cover double that space. *Forget bumping into the boat,* Colt thought. *We're going to bump right into a dinosaur instead...*

They were coming up to the back of the boat and he was relieved to see that Heath and Nyoko had managed to navigate the raft so that they were going to miss the side and the edge of the boat altogether. That was good in that they would not strike it, but bad in that he was going to really have to reach to grab that ladder...a ladder that he was now starting to realize was going to be over his head.

"Give me the oar," he said.

He saw that Heath and Nyoko, still holding the oar as a team, had spotted the *Cryptoclidus*, which was now so close to them that he could see beyond its humps in the water. He could see the length of it, stretching out, its head somewhere in the water directly beside them.

"Hey," Colt snapped. "Give me the damned oar or we're going to miss the boat!"

Quickly, Heath gave Colt the oar just as they were coming up along the backside of the boat. Although the thing was not running, it still took up considerable space with its weight and Colt was surprised to find that it still managed to create a wake, albeit a minor one. As they came to the back, Colt dipped the oar in and fought his way around, trying to angle himself as close to the ladder as he could.

When he was close enough to at least *try* his idea, he stopped stroking at the water and jabbed the oar upwards over his head like a spear. He missed the ladder the first time, but the second attempt worked; he wedged the end of the oar between the first and second rung, pressing it against the boat and trapping it between the rungs of the ladder.

"Nyoko, you go first," Colt said.

She nodded and came to him, but it was clear that she was petrified. She came to the edge of the raft and stood up on the side. The shifting of the raft nearly made Colt lose his footing, but he managed to keep himself up by pulling on the oar.

He heard a light crack from the plastic length of it that made his heart hammer in his chest.

Nyoko grabbed the bottom run and, with a boost from Colt's free hand, was able to plant a foot along the side of the boat and start climbing up. When she had made it up several rungs, Heath came next. He stepped up on the side of the raft and reached up, his eyes looking not to the ladder, but to the humps of the *Cryptoclidus*.

And that's when another part of it breached the surface.

Its head came up, its neck long and thick. It was very similar to the plesiosaur that many people believed the Lochness Monster to be, but a bit wider and gentler looking. Its neck and head towered at least twelve feet over the raft, and for the time being, it seemed more interested in the Princess Celeste than the humans in the life raft.

"Go now..." Colt whispered to Heath, hoping that the *Cryptoclidus* would spend its time worried with the massive steel intruder in its waters long enough to allow them to get up the ladder. For now, that seemed to be the case. It prodded at the side of the ship in a way that reminded Colt of how a cat will often rub against a new leg, seeking affection. He was pretty sure that if they were to get hurt by this beast, it would not be out of any violent tendencies but sheer curiosity.

Heath was far enough up the ladder where Colt could now finally grab the bottom rung. He had to stretch out to grab it, and when he did, he lost his grip on the oar. Still, it remained wedged between the ship and the ladder. Using the side of the ship for leverage, Colt made it up to the next rung and then the next. He looked up ahead of him and saw that Heath was two rungs up and, from what he could tell, Nyoko had nearly made it to the end of the ladder and the edge of the secondary deck.

Colt was reaching up for the next rung on the ladder when a loud thumping noise from his right distracted him. He turned in that direction and froze in mid-grasp. The *Cryptoclidus* was still nuzzling the side of the ship, but it had come closer. Beneath Colt's feet, down in the water, its body had struck the raft and overturned it. And now the dinosaur was looking curiously at Colt. Its head was no more than five feet from Colt. Its eyes looked bright and intelligent, and there was something overall kind about it. Still, knowing that its mouth was easily large enough to devour him in one bite was terrifying. Colt stared at it for another few seconds, mesmerized, and then slowly started to make his way up the ladder. He moved the tiniest bit he could, even when he had grabbed the rung above him and pulled himself up. He moved slowly but deliberately, not wanting to alarm the *Cryptoclidus*.

From above, he heard Heath mutter an "*Oh shit*," as he looked down to check on him.

That's putting it lightly, Colt thought as he continued to move slowly upward. As he made it to another rung and started to pull up, the *Cryptoclidus* gave a soft chuffing sound and then turned away. It slowly descended down into the water, and Colt watched as it eventually disappeared altogether.

Colt let out an exasperated sigh and didn't realize just how tense he had been in the minute or so he had been in the beast's gaze. Feeling roughly one thousand pounds lighter, Colt continued up the ladder and joined Nyoko and Heath on the gloriously sturdy floor of the ship's secondary deck.

TEN

In the same way Colt assumed astronauts must feel the first time they take a spacewalk—whether it be on the moon or repairing a telescope or the International Space Station—he got what he was sure was a similar feeling when he stepped foot onto the *Princess Celeste*. For a moment, the unreal instant where he had stared into the *Cryptoclidus*'s eyes was forgotten; he was standing on a myth, a relic of paranormal folklore.

"You okay?" Nyoko asked him.

"As well as to be expected," Colt said. "On small step for man and all that. How about you, Heath?"

"With the exception that I just watched a man climb up a ladder about five feet away from a living breathing dinosaur, I guess I'm doing pretty good."

"We need to find the communications room," Nyoko said, already heading down the walkway of the deck.

"I'm pretty sure the chances are slim that anything in the communications room on this ship still works," Colt said.

"I'm well aware of that," Nyoko said. "But, it's a good place to start."

She was still in a sour mood, and as they slowly made their way across the ship, Colt thought he understood it. Nyoko was used to being in control. She was the type of woman that stayed three steps ahead of any given situation. But in their current predicament, that was impossible. She had no control here, no game plan, and it was getting under her skin.

They walked down the secondary deck and came to the end where a single large door opened up onto the ship's interior. They found themselves standing in an empty lobby area. A few decorative chairs were scattered here and there, most of them overturned. The entire place had a film of dust on everything. The red ornamental carpet was dingy and discolored, making everything within the ship appear to be muted.

Ahead of them, a flight of stairs built into the wall led further down into the ship while one directly beside it, separated by a decorative golden rail, led up.

"Any idea where the communications room would be?" Nyoko asked.

"My guess," Heath said "is that it would be near the captain's quarters. So probably upstairs near the galley."

They shared an uncomfortable glance, waiting for someone to take the lead into the abandoned ghost ship that awaited them.

"Oh come on," Colt said, finally taking the lead and heading for the stairs. Truth be told, he was fine with the role. He'd made a career out of leading people into dark and unexplainable places. Why should this be any different?

Up the stairs, they came to a smaller version of the lobby they had entered in upon. It led to a set of double doors that were partially open, revealing the bridge. They ventured into it and found it as desolate and neglected as the rest of the ship. Colt looked out of the large window to the sea beyond. He found himself looking for the *Cryptoclidus* again, but there were no signs of it.

He turned his attention to Nyoko as she experimentally toggled switches and pushed buttons that he was totally unfamiliar with. She let out a nervous sigh and looked out to the ocean, defeat in her eyes. She looked towards a small adjoining room, connected by a small wooden door. A square window sat in the middle of the door, revealing a few pieces of equipment that even Colt could tell had something to do with communications. There was a very old-style CB radio (or so he guessed that's what it was) hanging on the wall.

"You think it's even worth checking?" he asked, opening the door.

"No," she said. "Everything is dead."

Colt tried anyway, walking into the communications room and testing the mic. There was an old dial embedded into the dashboard within the room. He turned it this way and that but, the needle within the tuning glass remained flat on the left side, unmoving.

"Well," he said, dropping the radio mic and letting it dangle. "At least we aren't out on the water in a raft with a dinosaur facing us."

Nyoko turned around and looked back out through the small lobby behind them. "I guess we just need to look the boat over for anything that might help us."

"Help us *what?*" Heath asked.

"For now…just to survive in case we're here for a long period of time."

It wasn't a possibility that Colt had thought about, but once it was out of Nyoko's mouth, it seemed all too real. They had been transported to what was apparently a prehistoric era and were trapped on a passenger ship that had gone missing more than seventy years ago. And they might very well never make it off. Even if they did, they'd then need to figure out how to get back to their time.

But they could figure all of that out later. For now, things needed to be taken one step at a time.

They walked in a single file line, with Colt still in front, to explore the rest of the ship. They headed back down to the lobby they had entered in from the secondary deck on and then walked down the stairs. The further down they went, the darker the ship became. Small windows were placed along the ship's sides, giving them at least *some* sort of dingy light.

The third floor consisted of two hallways that ran the length of the ship. Colt counted thirty doors on each side, leading into identical rooms. Each room had a bed, a small closet, and a tiny bathroom. Each room was empty, one just as dead the next.

"Anyone else creeped out yet?" Heath asked as they reached the end of the hallway. "If the ship disappeared, shouldn't the bodies of the people that went missing with the ship be on here somewhere?"

"That makes sense," Colt said. "And it also makes me *really* not want to go exploring down below."

But of course, that's where they went next. The next floor, which seemed to be the final level other than the boiler room and storage, consisted of what looked to be a large ballroom with a dining room adjoined to it. In the back of the dining room, through a large swinging door, was the kitchen. Everything looked clean but, at the same time, overwhelmingly neglected.

As they walked into the kitchen, each and every footfall seemed to echo. It was by far the most haunting part of the ship so far because there was very little light down here. They walked through what was slightly darker than twilight as they headed back out into the dining room.

It was then that they saw the two figures standing on the other side of the door. In the murky light of the dining room, they looked haunting. Still, it was something of a relief to see other people here. To Colt, though, there was one huge question that needed to be answered before he decided if he was happy to see them or…well, or something else.

Were they original passengers of the *Princess Celeste?*

"When did you get here?" one of the figures asked abruptly.

From across the fifty feet of the dining room, it was hard to see any real definition to either of the figures. The one that had spoken was clearly a man, given the sound of his voice. Colt thought the slight curves of the other one indicated that it was likely a woman, but he wasn't sure.

"About half an hour ago," Nyoko said, stepping in front of Colt and Heath. Colt let her do it and was glad to do so. This was *her* expedition, so he was more than happy to let her take control whenever she wanted. "How about you?" she added.

The figures were silent for a moment, but the man called back across the dining room after a few tense moments. "We aren't sure," he said.

"Maybe two weeks," his companion said. Colt had been correct; it was a woman.

Nyoko started walking forward, making sure to go slowly. Colt followed behind her and noticed that the two people standing at the dining room door were staying put. He sometimes forgot that not everyone was as accustomed to weirdness as he was. Not everyone willingly walked *towards* the unexplained so openly. If these people had been here for two weeks all alone on a ghost ship, he could only imagine how terrified they must be to all of a sudden find three more people wandering around.

"My name is Nyoko," she said as she drew closer. "The men behind me are Colt McKinnon and Heath Francis. We're likely here for different reasons, but I assure you...we're just as scared and confused as you are."

"I find that doubtful," the woman said.

The man finally took a step forward, and when he started introducing himself, they were nearly all standing together inside the doorway. "I'm Tyler Geller," the man said. "And this is my wife, Anne."

"How did you guys end up here?" Colt asked.

"We were on a yacht," Anne Geller answered. "We were out for out anniversary, just sort of cruising around."

"We hit rough water," Tyler said. "And then…I don't even know how to explain what happened after that."

"Something that looked like a storm, right?" Heath asked. "It came out of nowhere and by the time you were in the middle of it, it was too late. At some point, the clouds probably took on a yellow-ish color. You felt almost weightless for a minute and then everything sort of settled down. That sound about right?"

Both of the Gellers looked at him as if they were expecting him to grow a second head. Colt wasn't sure if he would have gone after them in such an abrupt way, but at least it was out there in the open now. There would be no pretending that there was nothing out of the ordinary going on here.

"That sounds exactly right," Anne said. "You just left out the part about the monsters."

"What monsters?" Colt asked.

"Out in the water," Tyler said. "Massive things. Like a dragon."

The dining room was quiet for a minute before Colt decided to try to take up Heath's method of conversation. "When you were on the yacht…you know where you were, right?"

Tyler laughed nervously. "We joked about it on the second day out to sea," he said. "We joked how our love was braving the Bermuda Triangle. It doesn't seem that funny now…"

"How'd you guys end up here?" Anne asked.

"We're sort of here on purpose," Nyoko said. "We're a small team of specialists that flew out over the Triangle to get some readings. I'm trying to better understand how the anomalies work."

"And did you run into a storm, too?" Anne asked.

"Yes," Heath said. "We sort of crashed the plane into the ocean. We were on a life raft for about two hours before this ship came into view."

"And the monsters?" Tyler asked. "Did you see them?"

"We saw something *like* monsters," Heath said.

"We believe we're in a prehistoric era," Nyoko said.

"The monster we saw was called a *Cryptoclidus*," Colt told them. "It's a dinosaur that lived in the seas during the Jurassic period."

"Are you kidding us right now?" Tyler asked.

"Not at all," Colt said.

"Well, I find it hard to believe we're in a prehistoric ocean," Anne said. "Mainly because every piece of information we've found around here is dated 1945."

Colt frowned and felt himself slipping into the role of the supernatural expert that always tried to break news gently. "I assume you don't have a deep knowledge of the Bermuda Triangle, do you?" he asked.

"No," Anne said. She sounded almost irritated with him. "Other than the fact that we are apparently stuck on a ghost ship from the 1940s, I know *nothing* about the Bermuda Triangle."

"Well, the ship we're on is called the *Princess Celeste,*" Colt said. "It went missing in 1945…in the Bermuda Triangle."

"Then why is there no one on the ship?" Tyler asked. Colt was relieved to find that he saw very little disbelief on the man's face.

"I don't know the answer to that."

"But you said you three were trying to get readings, right?" Anne said. "Does that mean you're some sort of scientists?"

"Sort of," Colt said.

"Yes, we are," Nyoko said, casting Colt an annoyed looked.

"So then, do you know how we can get the hell off of this ship and back home?"

"Not yet," Nyoko said. "But I plan to bust my ass trying to figure it out."

ELEVEN

The Gellers led them back up to the third floor and to one of the sixty boarding rooms. There was barely enough room for all five of them to stand inside, so Colt remained slightly outside of the doorway.

"We were in here when we heard you guys walking in from the deck up above," Anne said. "Hearing footsteps on a ship that was clearly abandoned for more than seventy years makes you a little jumpy. We hid from you until we were pretty sure you were harmless."

"You've been bunking in here for two weeks?" Nyoko asked.

"Yeah."

"What happened to the yacht?" Heath asked.

"The storm was too rough," Tyler said. "It started taking on water not even ten minutes after the storm passed. It eventually tipped over almost completely on its side, but we were able to make it here before it sank completely. We were fortunate in that when the clouds cleared, this ship was not even a quarter of a mile away. We made it to ship and climbed up the ladder along the back just as the yacht *really* started to sink."

"It was our twentieth anniversary," Anne said a little sweetly. "Getting out on the open water is just something we've always wanted to do. Tyler had had his license for about a three years now, and it was actually a lot of fun for those two days."

Anne smiled at the recollection, reaching under the small bed that was bolted into the wall. She pulled out two backpacks and a small duffel bag. "This was all that we were able to salvage from the yacht before it sank. We've had to ration our food because, as you can see, there wasn't much."

The direness of the Geller's situation hit Colt hard for the first time. They had a few bottles of water, a box of snack crackers, three apples and a single banana that was now almost completely brown. He saw a few empty wrappers to snack cakes and three empty bottles of water in with the food and tried to imagine what it must be like to have to ration such paltry supplies while starting to believe that they might very well die here.

"So, as you can tell from our meager supplies," Tyler said, "we're a little anxious to get the hell off of this ship."

Anne smiled, but it was a tired one that made her look older than the forty or forty-five years that Colt thought she might be. "It's not as bad as it seems," she said. "We had two bottles of wine, a block of cheese, and some grapes that we managed to stretch out for about a week. With no working refrigerator, it was tricky."

"I'm going to be honest," Nyoko said. "For now, I have no real ideas about what to do. But to start, I'd like to get a look at some of the information you came across where you figured out the date of the ship's voyage. I can't help but wonder if there are some sort of instructions on how to get a back-up communication system going."

"Even if there is," Heath said, "would it make any difference? If we're somewhere in prehistoric times, who's going to answer us?"

Colt had been thinking the same thing but knew not to say anything. Nyoko's mood finally seemed to be improving, and he was not about to set her off on a funk again.

"Can you just show us where it is anyway?" Nyoko asked.

"Certainly," Anne said. "But most of it is down with the engines. And there's hardly any light down there. It can get a bit spooky."

"I think we can handle that," Colt said.

The Gellers led them back downstairs to the ballroom. Colt tried to imagine people eating and dancing within the room, and it made him feel like a ghost himself, haunting a space that had been long abandoned.

To the far side of the room was a metal door with a sign on the wall beside it, reading AUTHORIZED PERSONNEL ONLY. They entered this door and stepped out into a thin hallway that went on for several carpeted feet before it came to a small flight of stairs. A single window ran along this hallway, shining light down into the stairs. The stairway was in much worse shape than anything else they had seen on the boat. The gloom below looked thick even before they made it to the stairs.

"Before we go down there," Tyler said, "I think there might be one other thing we should tell you. I'm only mentioning it now because you three seem to know a good deal about what might be going on here. And, quite frankly, if there are *dinosaurs* involved now...well, nothing can sound as crazy as I'm thinking it does."

"I happen to specialize in crazy," Colt said. "What is it?"

"Well, we were here for five days when we heard the first airplane. We ran outside to the deck, hoping to wave it down for help, but I don't think it saw us. More than that...well, it...it disappeared. It didn't fly out of sight or go behind a cloud or anything like that. The damned thing just winked out of being."

"What kind of plane?" Nyoko asked. "Was it one that looked like it was from the 40s or a modern one?"

"It looked like a modern fighter jet almost," Tyler said.

"We've seen them twice," Anne added. "Both times, they were in the same place. It was a different plane each time—you could tell from the color—but they were in the exact same place."

"I have no idea what it means, but it made us feel even worse," Tyler said. "It was almost like we were ghosts that those planes couldn't see. But then the planes disappeared, and it made us feel…helpless, I guess. It made us feel like even if there *was* a hope of being rescued, it was out of our hands. That it might be almost impossible."

"Also," Anne added, "there have been a few particularly violent storms since we've been here. They happen almost exactly the way you explained the same storm that seems to have brought us here. They come out of nowhere and are pretty rough. We've seen lighting during a few of them, and the waves get pretty ferocious."

"How many have there been since you've been here?" Colt asked.

"Five, I think," Anne said.

Tyler nodded in agreement.

"Any idea how long they lasted?" Nyoko asked.

"It varies," Tyler answered. "One of them was over within less than five minutes. But then one of them—the first one that passed through, in fact—seemed to go on forever. Maybe five or six hours. It rocked this ship so much that Anne got a little sick. The last one came through three days ago and was maybe about an hour or so."

"You mentioned you guys seeing the dinosaurs," Colt said. "Only, you referred to them as monsters. When did you see them?"

"A few times now, when we go to sit on the deck, hoping to see a plane or another boat," Tyler said. "They'll sort of just surface every now and then, you know? We've never had anything attack the ship, though. I guess it's big enough to be intimidating."

"Count yourself lucky," Colt said. "I had a pretty close encounter with a *Cryptoclidus* coming on the ship."

"A what?" Tyler asked.

"Long neck, looks sort of like the Lochness Monster."

"Oh," Tyler said, clearly dumfounded.

With a visible shake in his step, Tyler led the way down the stairs with Anne clinging closely to him. Colt trailed behind them with Nyoko and Heath close behind. Similar to the kitchen, their footfalls echoed like thunder as they descended the stairs. It did not take long for the darkness of the engine room to take over. The place seemed to have been thrown into some weird eternal dusk. The smell of neglected steel and oil only added to the ethereal feel of the place.

Colt was impressed with the engines. It was almost like walking through a museum; everything was perfectly preserved and untouched. But knowing that he was in the bowels of the heralded *Princess Celeste* was also sort of creepy. Looking at the pistons and motors all aligned perfectly was like some strange form of poetry. He couldn't even start to imagine the stories and lives that all coiled around the creation of this ship.

About halfway through the engine room, there was a large beam that ran up from the floor to the ceiling. There were a few clipboards on it, all containing a similar form. The only terminology on them that Colt understood was *Engine Check*. Underneath a dozen or so terms were little squares that made up a checklist of sorts. At the top of each chart, there was a space for a name and a date. Colt looked at all of the clipboards—nine in all—and saw that each had last been dated October 02, 1945. He thumbed through old charts behind the one on the top and saw that they only went back to January 12, 1945.

"Yeah, that was the first thing we saw, too," Anne said. "But then we found this…"

She stepped around to the backside of the column and knelt down. The back of the column was apparently hollow, or at least the bottom of it was. She pulled out a black box that looked to be roughly the size of a small suitcase. The box was made of metal and had a concave top that was recessed into the box by about six inches. Inside this was something that looked very much like a built-in laptop. He even saw what appeared to be a USB port. He saw what he thought was likely a power button and pushed it. The box did not respond.

"Any idea what this is?" he asked Nyoko.

She eyed it suspiciously and shook her head. "No. But there's no way in hell this was something that existed in 1945."

"We didn't think so, either," Tyler said.

Colt studied the thing a bit more, frowning. "You know, Nyoko," he said. "This might mean that you aren't the first one to venture into the Bermuda Triangle for scientific study."

"It wouldn't surprise me," she said. "Do you mind lugging it topside to see if I can figure it out?"

"Your wish is my command," he said.

"Well, this isn't all," Tyler said. "There's something else that I'm pretty sure *will* prove that other people have been out here."

"Where?" Heath asked.

"This way."

Tyler led them deeper into the engine room. As they reached the back, where there was almost no light at all, they came to a small closet-like space. It was tucked away on the side opposite the engines.

Always thinking, Nyoko pulled her cellphone out of her pocket and used it as a flashlight. The light shone inside, revealing a small workspace. A tiny desk contained several file folders, an old laptop, and two portable hard drives. And although it all looked just as untouched as the rest of the ship, the materials were clearly much more recent than 1945.

"What the hell is going on?" Heath asked.

Colt looked to Nyoko and saw that she was smiling. It was the smile he had come to know well—the smile that meant she had some work to do and could not wait to get started. And just like that, her bad mood was gone, and she looked like a jubilant little girl racing to the presents under a Christmas tree on Christmas morning.

"Colt, you guys see if you can come up with some way to get off of this ship," she said. "I think I'm going to be busy for a while."

TWELVE

Colt couldn't help but feel a little weird about leaving Nyoko alone down in the engine room. Sure, when she was with electronics of any kind, she was sort of in her own little playground, but the place just reeked of things forgotten. He gave her a last glance as he followed the Gellers back through the engine room and then she was gone.

A chill crept through him, but he managed to look past it, focusing more on the task at hand: survival and getting off of this freaky ghost ship.

When they were back in the ballroom, Colt felt as if he had been in a cave and was just now surfacing for air. The pressing weight of the engine room slid right off, and he felt himself relax considerably.

"Are there no lifeboats anywhere on board?" Colt asked.

"There are a few," Anne said.

"We've considered trying to use them," Tyler added. "But honestly…getting into the water with those monsters out there…it just didn't seem smart. We were going to use it as a last resort kind of thing for when food started to run low. We figured it was safer to just stay on here and hope someone might come by and rescue us."

"Makes sense to me," Heath said.

"Me, too," Colt said. "But the fact that those planes that come through seem to be disappearing makes me think that there isn't a very good chance of being rescued by one."

"And what's your idea?" Anne asked, sounding a bit insulted.

"I don't think you'll care much for it," Colt said. "But maybe we should go check out those lifeboats before we get ahead of ourselves."

The Gellers led Colt and Heath back up through the ship, to the central lobby. From there, they walked out to the secondary deck and headed to the front of the boat. The ocean was tranquil, slapping gently at the side of the ship. Colt looked out again, hoping to catch a glimpse of some other prehistoric marvel. But for now, there was nothing to see—just the constantly churning water sitting under a placid blue sky.

At the front of the boat, lined up in rows of three and stacked four high, were the lifeboats. By simply looking at them, Colt saw where a few of them wouldn't be of use. Time and the elements had deteriorated their wooden exteriors. Working together, Colt, Heath, and Tyler Geller unstacked them, sliding the useless ones off of the metal racks that held them up. They were left with four that were in good shape, having rested under their useless copies for over seventy years.

"Well, at least we know we have a boat to use," Colt said. "Anyone have any idea how to get them down into the water?"

"I'm guessing this," Heath said, kicking at a series of ropes that were tucked behind the metal rack. "I'm pretty sure you attach the boat to the rope and lower it down. That's how it was done on the *Titanic,* anyway."

"Not the best nautical reference right now," Colt said. "But thanks."

"And just who will stay up here to lower it down?" Anne asked.

"We'll cross that bridge when we get there," Colt said.

"And you're fine with floating around on the water without any real idea of how to get back home?" Tyler asked.

"No, I'm not okay with it. But I also don't like the idea of waiting for help that probably won't come on a ship that has been floating around in the same region of water for just shy of a century."

At first, Tyler looked as if he wanted to argue the point but he eventually nodded. "Yeah, that makes sense. You have to remember, though, that we had no idea what this ship had been through. To think that it's been here, trapped in time, for all those years…"

"And what about the people that were on it?" Heath asked. "Where the hell did they all go?"

"Okay, enough of that," Anne said, hugging herself and trying to suppress a chill. "Please."

"So we're really going to do this?" Tyler asked, running his hand along the edge of the boat they had chosen.

"That's the plan," Colt said. Although, really, he wasn't sure yet.

Nyoko had come out into the Triangle, putting her life at risk, in the hopes of learning what she could about what went on inside the Triangle when it was active. Her laptop had died on her while still in the air, and Colt had no idea how much of that information had remained. If Nyoko wasn't satisfied with the amount of information she had gathered, he wasn't sure if she would leave so easily. Hopefully, she was finding out all she could from the equipment down below…if she had been able to get them to work.

With the best of the useful boats selected, Heath tied the rope to the steel pivot points that were located at the front and the rear of the boat. He then attached it back to the rack and, after a few minutes of their group trying to figure out how to get it to move along the rack, they had it positioned and ready to go.

With that done, they headed back to the third floor and returned to the Geller's room. As the Gellers started to pack up their things, Colt's thoughts once again returned to Nyoko. He really did not like the idea of her being in that engine room alone.

"Do me a favor," he said, stepping out into the hallway. "You guys hang here for a while. Let me have a talk with Nyoko."

"You okay?" Heath said.

"Yeah. I just want to make sure she's on the same page as we are. I want to make sure she's putting the need to escape this place above her need for data."

Anne Geller looked a little off put by this. "Would she really stay here longer just to hope to get more information?"

"I don't think so," Colt lied. "But I just want to see. I've worked with her for a while now, and I'd like for any awkward or tense conversations to take place between me and her rather than all five of us."

Colt didn't wait for a response. He headed back down the hall and then took the stairs to the large ballroom. When he entered the door that would take him to the engine room, he once again felt like he was descending down into a mine or cavern of some kind. Less than forty-five minutes had transpired since they had left Nyoko down there, but it seemed like much longer than that.

He made it down into the engine room and was relieved to hear the sound of Nyoko's delicate fingers striking at a keyboard. It sounded almost like a robotic scurrying down in the depths of the ship. When he came to the small room, he knocked on the already-opened door, not wanting to startle her.

She turned to him and frowned. "Where's everyone else?"

"In the Geller's room, packing up. We found a lifeboat that should hold up pretty well. Once the Gellers get their things together, we're good to go."

"Sounds good."

"Are you okay with leaving here without reams of information?"

She shrugged and got to her feet. As she approached him, Colt saw that she had taken her own laptop out of its case and had one of the portable hard drives connected to it.

"Yes," she said. "I think once we crashed into the ocean, I was fine with getting back home with whatever I had. That crash scared me more than I care to admit."

"Yeah, I could tell. You okay now?"

"Yeah. Getting behind the computer and doing something useful has really helped."

"Did you find anything useful?" he asked.

"Not useful, but very interesting."

"Like what?"

Nyoko chuckled a bit and turned back to the desk. "This sort of information is the kind of stuff my grandfather would have salivated over. I wasn't able to start the laptop that was here; the battery is dead, and there's no outlet to charge it. However, I used my own cables and was able to pull up both portable hard drives on my computer."

"What was on them?"

"Well, the first one was nothing but a bunch of report templates and numerical data that I didn't understand. So I saved all of that to my laptop to study later; I used the portable WiFi hotspot to transfer it all to the cloud. This other one, though, is full of information that some might consider juicy. There are write-ups, detailed reports, and what looked to be drafts of letters. We're talking about stuff from the Army, the Navy, the NSA, and on and on."

"And it's just been sitting here?" Colt asked. "All this time?"

"Well, that's where it gets tricky." She pulled up a file on her laptop and then pointed to the top of the screen. Colt saw what looked to be a formal report of some kind, and it was dated as April 20, 1996.

"How can that be?" he asked.

"Well, I plan on taking these two hard drives with me, so you can look it all over some other time. But I'll give you the gist for right now. The U.S. government has been studying the anomalies within the Bermuda Triangle since 1939, ever since they lost seven boats and two fighter jets undergoing training exercises. According to what I was able to find on these hard drives, the government first officially visited this side of the Triangle—what they called *'being transported'*—in November of 1942."

"That's…incredible."

"It gets better," Nyoko said. "They discovered the *Princess Celeste* for the first time in September of 1947. They knew the ship for what it was right away because it had disappeared in these waters in '45. They came aboard and saw no sign of the passengers or crew. They somehow managed to come back to this exact spot more than twenty times between 1948 and 1970. There's a blank period after that but then there are reports from 1991. There are reports from the same man—a Crosby Delocroix—that go on until 1996. His last report indicates that he heard screaming and when he went topside to check it out, he saw lifeboats with the passengers and crew of the *Princess Celeste*. But before he could even think to offer help, they disappeared."

"So the government has been using this place as a base of sorts?" Colt asked.

"Seems like it. And it gives us some hope because it basically states that somehow, there *is* a way in and out of here. They mention the lightning storms here and there in regards to energy resources and atmospheric anomalies. They were working on getting experimental crafts out here to ride the storms out and test the storms and the energy they seem to carry."

"Yeah, I figured the storms would be important," Colt remarked.

"Also, all throughout these reports, they mention seeing dinosaurs out in the water. From what I can tell, they saw their first one in 1952. After that, there are whole sections within the reports specifically pertaining to dinosaurs that they had spotted in the waters. I saw references to *Nothosaurus, Cryptoclidus, Elasmosaurus*, and then ones listed as 'other.'"

"So to have them listed so professionally, do you think they had an actual paleontologist out here?" Colt asked.

"It wouldn't surprise me. Hell, you have access to what can basically be called working time travel *and* access to living dinosaurs. I'm pretty sure they put every available resource they had on this. The last report is from '96, but if this was a base of operations that could have been kept operational, there's no end to the knowledge that could be gained."

"And you're taking the hard drives?"

"Yeah. I can't see where these things have been used for nearly twenty years. I think if whoever was using them wanted them, they wouldn't be here. I think someone *planned* to come back and use them but never made it."

"I wonder why," Colt said.

"I don't know," Nyoko said. "But when you have time travel and dinosaurs tied up into on big knot, I don't think I want to sit around and hope to find out."

"So you ready to go?"

"Yes," she said. "But before we just plop down in the ocean, I think we need to wait for one of those storms to come along. It seems pretty obvious that those are the key. If we have any chance of getting back home, I think we need to ride out one of those storms."

"Yeah, I'm thinking the same thing. The Gellers seem a little shaky, though. I don't know how they're going to feel about purposefully trying to row one of those lifeboats into a storm."

"How about you?" she asked, again turning away from the computers. "How are you holding up?"

Colt gave a shaky laugh. "I'm elated and terrified all at once. It's kind of crazy. But I do think we need to wait for one of those storms before getting in the water. If there are reoccurring sightings of dinosaurs in those reports, I think it's all the proof we need that the sea here isn't friendly."

"So, that's the plan then. We stay here until we hear one of those storms approaching and then get into the water. We head for wherever the storm is coming from and hope it takes us, just like it took the plane."

"For a plan, that really sucks," Colt joked.

"But it's all we have," Nyoko said. She looked back to her laptop and cracked her knuckles playfully. "Now, just let me finish up here, and we'll talk to the Gellers about it."

"How much time do you need?"

"Not long. Maybe another half an hour?"

"Sounds good," he said.

He turned to go back up but was stopped when Nyoko reached out and grabbed his hand. He turned back and saw that she was stepping towards him, and before he knew what was happening, she was kissing him. It caught him by surprise and caused him to lean back against the wall. He returned the kiss, and it became fairly heated. One of his hands found her hair while the other found her waist and pulled her closer to him. He tried to think of a time when they had kissed one another when sex was not going to be involved and came up empty.

That thought got swept away quickly, though. When his hands started to explore a bit too much, Nyoko broke the kiss and stepped away.

"Sorry," she said. "But I've been wanting that ever since the crash."

"No need to apologize," he said. He stayed there against the wall, waiting for his nerves to settle. "In fact, you *never* have to apologize for anything like that."

She smiled at him and then turned her attention back to the computer screen in front of her. Taking that as his final cue, Colt turned back to the engine room and headed back for Heath and the Gellers.

THIRTEEN

The last thing Colt had expected to see when he returned to the Geller's quarters was an assault rifle. But sure enough, there it was, on the bed like something out of a messed up museum. The Gellers and Heath were looking at it thoughtfully when Colt entered the room.

"Where'd that come from?" Colt asked.

"We found it down near the engine room on our first day here," Tyler said. "There were two handguns, too—basic Glocks, I think—but we never found any ammunition for them. This, though, has nine rounds loaded."

"Any idea what kind of gun it is?" Colt asked. He had never been interested in guns outside of enjoying them in action while watching a violent movie.

"No clue," Tyler said.

"Same here," Heath said. "I'm not much of a gun guy."

"Maybe Nyoko will know," Colt said. "She seems to know everything else."

"Speaking of which," Heath said, "are we going to have to drag her away kicking and screaming?"

"No. She's saving some data from those old laptops and she'll be up."

"I'm a little confused," Anne said. "What kind of scientists are you, exactly?"

"We're not scientists, really," Colt said. "At least, I'm not."

"This is Colt McKinnon," Heath said. "The guy that came off of Spectre Island. You haven't heard of him?"

The Gellers both looked apologetic but gave matching shakes of their heads. "Whatever you are," Tyler said, "do you feel confident that you can get us off of this boat?"

"I wouldn't say *confident,*" Colt said. "But we have a plan."

"We do?" Heath asked.

Before Colt could answer, Nyoko appeared in the doorway behind them. She was carrying her laptop bag and the expression on her face was a peculiar mix of excitement and fear. "Yes," she said. "We do. And I think we need to talk about it as a group because, quite frankly, it's going to sound nuts."

"How nuts?" Tyler asked.

She stepped into the room and presented the plan that she and Colt had briefly discussed downstairs. She also shared her findings with the rest of the group—about how the Princess Celeste had been used by the US military since the late 1930s as a way station of sorts to study the phenomenon of the Bermuda Triangle. With Colt's help, she stressed that the storms and peculiar lights in the sky seemed to have a direct correlation to what the military had referred to as *being transported.*

"So what I'm hearing," Anne said, "is that the only real plan we have is to drop ourselves in the sea on a rickety old lifeboat in the middle of an unpredictable storm and *hope* that we find our way back home. Is that about right?"

"Yes," Nyoko said. "And I have a pretty odd amount of data to back it up."

"Of course," Tyler said, "we're talking about government sources that probably had sturdy boats to endure the storms."

"That's likely the case, yes," Nyoko said.

"Don't get us wrong," Colt said. "We're not thrilled about our chances, but they beat the hell out of staying here and waiting to be rescued while food rations run out. This is something the three of us are going to do…and we'd love to have you come with us if you're willing to take the risk."

The Gellers exchanged an uncomfortable look that spoke volumes. "So we'd have to sit around and just wait for one of those storms to come around?"

"Yes," Nyoko said. "You said that when these storms come through, there's no real time estimate to go by, right? Some are brief, and some are very long?"

"That's right," Anne said. "But if you're looking for an average, I'd say about an hour and a half at most. Of course, it's hard to be certain because my watch doesn't work here."

Nyoko looked to her own watch. Colt peered at it over her shoulder and saw the little digital marks were still making no sense, flickering in random shapes.

"That's perfectly in line with what I pulled off of the laptops downstairs," Nyoko said. "The reports said that most of the storms tend to last between seventy and ninety-five minutes. There were a few that suggested some of them can last as long as a day, though."

"So that's our window to get off of the ship, into the water, and hopefully to whatever force will get us back to our time?" Heath asked.

"Yes. I mean, we're taking a risk because we could catch one of the storms that is gone within ten or fifteen minutes. But it's a chance we have to take, I think."

The silence within the room was thick and uncomfortable. It was obvious that they were all thinking the same thing: it was going to be an extremely difficult task. And in the end, it could all turn out to be for nothing.

"Would you mind giving us some time to think it over?" Tyler asked.

"Absolutely not," Nyoko answered. "We'll be up top, on the deck."

With that, Colt, Nyoko, and Heath made their exit. Colt looked back to the Gellers as he walked through the doorway and saw that Anne looked terrified to the point of being on the verge of tears.

They walked back down the corridor, towards the front of the ship. Colt was again astounded by just how empty and quiet it was. It made him feel like an intruder. It made him feel like he was walking through some slice of history that very few people knew about. He figured such a feeling might make some people feel special but for Colt, it made him want to get off of this boat as quick as possible.

FOURTEEN

"It's sort of weird, isn't it?" Heath asked.

They were looking out to the ocean, standing on the central deck. The water was peaceful and unblemished. Any trace of their crashed plane or lurking dinosaurs were nowhere to be seen.

"What's weird?" Colt asked.

"We're assuming that we're floating in the sea a couple hundred million years ago. But the ocean looks the same as it does 2016."

"Well, with the drastic exception of the marine life," Colt joked.

Colt actually didn't find Heath's observation all that weird, but he knew what Heath meant. Being misplaced out of time in such a way, Colt expected to feel different. But because they were stranded at sea (albeit with extinct monsters lurking in the depths below), nothing really felt all that different.

Aside from the phantom ship they were currently standing on, of course.

"Do you think they'll come with us?" Nyoko asked Colt.

Colt considered the question for a moment before answering. "I don't know. I'd like to think so. But Anne looked absolutely horrified at the idea of getting back into the water."

"They said they were had been out on the sea for their twentieth anniversary," Heath pointed out. "I think finishing out their lives together in the real world is going to be too much of a lure for them to chicken out and stay here."

"My God," Nyoko said. "Can you imagine going through something like that? The strain and the stress, I mean. It's one of those things that will either draw them closer together or cause a lot of arguments. I feel bad for them."

Heath looked out to the sea and gave a weak laugh. "Yeah, me too. But I feel a bad for *us* more than that. Sorry of that sounds selfish."

"So what about our plan?" Colt asked. "Anyone else nervous about it?"

"Hell yes I am," Heath said. "Even if we can manage to get the lifeboat in the water easily, that still means that we have to get it to the source of the lights in an hour and a half. Depending on where the lights are—*if* there are any lights at all—that could be impossible."

"Yeah, that's the one flaw I see, too," Nyoko said.

"*One* flaw?" Heath asked with a shaky laugh.

"Isn't this what you signed up for?" Colt asked. "You're back in the Triangle, trapped again. How does it feel?"

"Not great."

The sound of footfalls from behind interrupted them. They turned to see the Gellers walking towards them from out of the main doorway back into the ship. They were holding hands, and it looked like Anne had been weeping.

"We talked it out," Tyler said, "and decided that we'd like to come with you."

"That's great," Colt said.

"But the one thing I ask that you keep in mind," Tyler said, "is that Anne comes first. No matter what happens when we're out there or what sort of danger we might face, I'll rescue Anne before I even think of helping you."

"And the same goes for me," Anne said. When she spoke, she would not look them in the eyes.

Colt thought he'd heard an undercurrent of resentment in Tyler's voice. Colt was pretty sure he understood: Tyler was angry that they had come to the ship today and presented them with this sudden plan, based on facts that they had not possessed before today. Rescue was great, but being faced with such a tremendous decision when it had not been expected was horrifying.

"That's perfectly understandable," Nyoko said.

"So now what?" Anne asked.

"Now," Nyoko said, "we wait for one of those ferocious storms to come through. Any idea when the last one was?"

"Yesterday morning," Tyler said. "And they probably rear up in some capacity about every two days or so. Sometimes it's much more frequent, though."

"A couple of days ago," Anne said, "there were three in one day."

"How about the planes?" Colt asked. "When they have showed up, was it directly before or after one of the storms?"

Tyler furrowed his brow and looked up to the sky, as if remembering the planes. "You know," he said, "I never even put that together. Both times we've seen the planes have been within an hour or so of the storms passing."

"I think that settles it then," Nyoko said.

"Yeah, that proves it as far as I'm concerned," Heath said.

"Well then," Tyler said. "We should probably pack up. The storms come out of nowhere, so we won't have much time to prepare."

Without another word spoken between them, they headed back inside. As they did, Colt looked to the sky and tried to gauge the time. If he had to make a guess, he'd say it was around four or five in the afternoon. While that timescale varied a bit from the scale they had been living by as they had taken the rental plane into the air, he was also sure that timescales were probably very tumultuous in the Bermuda Triangle.

As they walked back down into the hallway where the cabins were located, Tyler gestured to the doors all around them. "All of these rooms are unlocked," he said. "If we're going to be doing nothing more than waiting for a storm, you guys might as well grab a room and wait it out. Please don't take this the wrong way, but Anne and I would very much like to be left alone right now. This whole situation…it's just draining."

The three newcomers nodded their understanding as the Gellers headed off further down the hallway towards their room.

"Well, I don't know about you kids," Heath said to Colt and Nyoko, "but I'm going to do some exploring. This is just a little too cool to resist."

"I'm thinking about doing the same thing," Colt said.

Nyoko had already opened one of the doors to an empty cabin and looked inside. "I'm going to go through some of the information I found downstairs. I think it's a good idea if we all meet back here before dark."

"Sounds good," Heath said.

Heath started back for the top of the boat, Colt falling in behind him. He made no more than two steps before Nyoko called out: "Colt, can we talk for a second?"

"Sure," he said. He then looked back to Heath and said, "Don't get lost."

It was meant as a joke, but there was nothing resembling a smile on Heath's face as he started walking slowly away.

Colt and Nyoko entered the empty cabin. It felt stale and smelled like some long forgotten corner of a cellar. The bed was neatly made which, to Colt, was somehow the creepiest thing about the room. A she studied the bed, Nyoko sat down and instantly started to set up her laptop.

"You okay?" Colt asked.

"I think so," Nyoko said. "But I feel like there's something I need to let you know before we go riding into a massive storm on a lifeboat."

"Okay…" he said.

There was something in her voice that sounded vulnerable. And *vulnerable* was not usually a word that he would have ever associated with Nyoko.

"You know that I have spent most of my professional life behind computers and in labs, right?" she asked.

"Yes."

"Coming out to Spectre Island and accidentally rescuing you…well, that was my first real foray into adventure. And for the most part, that went smoothly for me. No real danger, no risks. But this whole thing today…from the helicopter crash to being chased by a creature straight out of time…I can't handle it."

Colt extended his hand to place on her shoulder, intending to comfort her. He'd never been in this role for her, as the strong one, the one that needed to have his shit together to make sure she made it through.

"What do you need?" he asked, taking the hand back, unsure of how to proceed.

"That's just it," she said. "I don't know. The easy answer—and one I am afraid and embarrassed to admit—is *you*. But that's not me. That's not *us*. We know what this thing between us is. It's work and sex. That's it. And it's great."

"It's better than great," Colt said. "It's awesome. But I think we know each other well enough where it can become something else if we need it to be…even if it's just for a while."

He then extended his hand again, placing it on her shoulder. Unexpectedly, Nyoko reached back and took it. It was easily the most intimate moment they'd ever shared, aside from the sex. But somehow, this was more personal, more meaningful. He drew her close and was amazed at how much it seemed to calm him.

"In the plane," Nyoko said. "After we crashed, you came right to me to make sure I was okay."

"Well, yeah. I saw that you were hurt."

"How did that make you feel?"

Colt wasn't sure how to answer and all of a sudden, he felt inadequate. He wasn't sure what exactly this powerful woman was expecting of him, but he was pretty sure he wouldn't be able to provide it.

"It made me afraid," he said. "I thought you'd been seriously hurt."

She turned to him, and he could see that she needed to hear something else. And while his heart was almost ready to say what she needed to hear, his tongue couldn't quite say it. Instead, he leaned down and kissed her. It was slow and deliberate, and there was something more than their usual heat in it. When he pulled away, her eyes were still closed. His hands moved as if of their own accord, and he cupped the side of her face, caressing her. He hadn't kissed a girl in that way since high school—the first girl he'd ever fallen in love with.

"We're going to be okay," he said. "We'll get out of this."

"It seems unlikely," she said.

"It does," he admitted. "But it also seemed very unlikely that I'd survive that island all those months ago. And I made it out."

"I guess you did," she said. "Although, you know, I had a little something to do with that."

"No, you had *a lot* to do with that," he said. "Apparently, we're a pretty good team."

She smiled, pulled his head down, and kissed him again. When she broke away, she said. "Yeah, I guess we are."

"We'll get out of this," he repeated.

She nodded and then gave him a playful shove away. "Alright. Go find Heath before he wanders off the boat."

"You got it, boss."

He exited the room and paused in the hallway, wondering what exactly had just happened. It had certainly been unexpected; it was the most emotion he had ever seen out of her and, quite frankly, it had rattled him. He let out a sigh and then headed back to the top of the boat in search of Heath.

When he was back outside in the open air, he looked back to the sky and saw that it was blue and crystal clear. There were no signs of a storm in sight. He then looked out to the ocean and saw the calm waters and the unreachable horizon.

Suddenly, Colt became very worried that they might be trapped here for good—that there would be no storm, and they would die here, slowly starving and quickly going crazy.

FIFTEEN

As Colt had assumed, the *Princess Celeste* offered no real clues as to what had happened to its original crew and passengers. He and Heath had spent the better part of an hour looking the place over, every inch of the ship feeling more and more like a long-forgotten haunted house. A few of the cabins had been in slight disarray, but there had been so signs of people trying to escape in a rush. They did not look through all of the rooms because almost all of them were identical; slight signs of occupation like unmade beds and crumpled mildewed towels, but nothing else. Similarly, if there had been any evidence of strange activity down below, it could only be found in the kitchen where some of the pots and pans that had been left out had accumulated mold that had long ago ceased to thrive.

Walking along the topside again, they did take note that a few of the lifeboats appeared to be missing, which jive with the report Nyoko had read about someone seeing a lifeboat filled with passengers heading for the ship before disappearing.

Somehow, the lack of evidence of a crew unsettled Colt more than anything else about the legendary ship. He was thinking of this as he and Heath headed back to the second floor. As they passed by the Gellers' cabin, they heard their muffled voices through the door. Colt heard Tyler's voice, doing his very best to sooth Anne. Colt had to fight the impulse to stop by and eavesdrop, trying to see what sort of worries and concerns they had. In the end, they gave the Gellers their privacy and headed further down the hallway.

"Can I ask you something?" Heath asked when the hushed voices of Anne and Tyler were behind them.

"Sure," Colt said.

"What's the deal with you and Nyoko?"

Colt shrugged. "Not much to tell," he lied. "It's a complicated working relationship."

"Sure it is," Heath said. "If you say so. All the same, I think I'm going to get my own cabin and let you two deal with your own rooming arrangements."

Colt didn't bother to deny the insinuation as Heath stopped by one of the cabins and opened the door. "Hopefully," Heath said, "there'll be a storm a-brewing the next time I see you."

"Yeah, let's hope so," Colt remarked. "See you then."

Heath closed the cabin door, leaving Colt alone in the hallway. He headed towards the cabin he knew Nyoko was still in and stopped in front of it. He nearly knocked on the door but, instead, decided to head topside again. It was immeasurably spooky to be walking alone in the empty ship, but it also allowed him to better sort his thoughts. It was the first time he had been alone since leaving the National Geographic offices. And although he *knew* that had only been yesterday afternoon, it felt like an imaginary day in another life.

Colt made his way to the deck and again found himself looking out to the ocean. He wondered what sort of creatures lurked below—both discovered by mankind in the future and undiscovered. Surely archeologists hadn't yet discovered every aquatic beast from prehistoric times. He thought of stories he'd read about the dreaded megalodon and other monsters that had once dominated the prehistoric sea. To be on a ship in those same waters was more than horrifying—it was humbling.

He glanced back to the sky, hoping to see some inkling of a storm on the way. But there was nothing...not a stray grey cloud, not a breeze that could potentially push a storm along, nothing.

"What are you thinking about?"

It was Nyoko's voice. Coming from behind him, it had startled him. It actually made him jump a bit, and he turned around to face her, slightly embarrassed.

"I'm thinking that I've never been out to sea and actually *hoped* for a storm to come along. Then again, I hadn't been stranded in the middle of the ocean before, either. So today is just full of firsts for me."

She nodded and looked out along with him. "Do you think this crazy plan will work?"

Colt shrugged. "Theoretically, it should. But hey...that's your specialty. I know squat abut magnetic shifts and all that nonsense."

It hit him at that moment that somehow, the power between the two of them had shifted. She had buckled for just a moment in the cabin, opening up to him, taking his hand and becoming vulnerable. He assumed that, to her, such an action was almost surrendering in a way. In a way, he thought the power shift had started right after the crash, when she had slipped into her helpless bad mood. Colt didn't want to call this out and make a big ordeal about it, so he tried to accept it as well as he could.

"I think it will all come down to the timing," she said.

"Yeah, we'll have to row our asses off. Against a storm, at that."

They were quiet for a moment, the only sound between them the slight splashing noises of the water lapping at the sides of the powerless ship.

"Colt, about what happened in the cabin..."

"No, not right now," he said. "Let's deal with one unprecedented situation at once. If we make it out of here alive, we can talk about that."

"Fine," she said with a smile. She actually looked rather relieved. "But in the meantime, can we resume our old habits?"

He didn't understand what she meant at first but then she hooked her index and middle fingers into the waist of his pants and pulled him back towards the deck exit, back towards the inside of the ship. It seemed odd to him—having sex with the knowledge that they may be marching towards their deaths anytime now—but who was he to argue?

"Yeah," he said. "I think we can do that."

They went back inside, leaving behind a perfectly clear sky and peaceful waters.

SIXTEEN

Colt opened his eyes to the sound of the small bed creaking. Sleeping on the mattress had been the equivalent of sleeping on a dusty slab of concrete, but he and Nyoko had fallen asleep without much problem after their lovemaking. It had been sort of slow and intense, a totally unexpected pace as compared to the way the usually handled things. Colt had fallen asleep wondering what these recent developments in their relationship might mean for them if they managed to get out of this alive.

Now, hearing her get out of bed, Colt sat up groggily. He opened his mouth to ask if she was okay, but he was interrupted by yet another sound before he could get the words out.

Thunder. It boomed outside and from within the cabin of the desolate ship, it sounded like a massive percussion drum placed directly above the ocean outside. As Colt stood up, he was also fairly certain he heard a roaring wind as well. It was a constant drone that was accompanied with muted splashing noises against the side of the *Princess Celeste.*

"That's our storm," Nyoko said. She was still naked, bending over to pick up her clothes from the floor. Colt started to do the same, hopping around in the small darkened room as the sounds of the storm picked up outside.

As he stepped into his boxer briefs, someone started pounding on the door. "Wake up," Heath was yelling on the other side. "We've got our storm!"

Colt, never really one to wake up quickly, tried his best to rouse himself. It did not take much, as the sounds outside were enough to wake anyone up. There was no light at all coming in through the cabin's window, indicating that it was night outside. That added an entirely new level of difficulty to their plan. But they could worry about that later, namely once they were in the water.

"Hey!" Heath kept shouting and pounding on the door. "Come on! Wake up!"

"We're awake," Nyoko called back, now slipping her shirt over her head.

Colt nearly fell over in the dark as he put his shoes on. He scrambled to the door, looked back to make sure Nyoko was fully clothed, and then opened the door. Heath stood there, eyes wide with anticipation. He looked terrified, but there was also a spastic energy in his expression.

Colt stepped out into the hallway and saw that Anne and Tyler were already rushing towards them. Tyler had two bags—a backpack slung over his shoulders and a small synch-sack which he carried by his side. The assault rifle that he'd had on the bed earlier was also slung over his shoulder.

"Everyone ready?" Colt asked.

"Yeah," Heath said.

"Do we have a choice?" Tyler asked.

Outside, thunder rolled yet again, as if beckoning them on. It echoed across the ship and sounded like some huge monster clearing its throat.

They raced to the end of the hallway, and as they neared the exit door for the deck, the storm grew louder. The wind was the loudest of all, punctuated by the occasional loud splash of the ocean against the side of the ship.

Heath reached the exit door first, pushing it open and leading them all outside. The night was shrouded in clouds, the wind pushing large storm clouds across the sky. There was the slightest drizzle of rain pelting down, blown in an almost diagonal pattern by the wind. They all took a moment to look to the sky and sea, gauging the conditions. For now, things didn't seem so bad. The most intimidating thing of all was the thunder. When it rumbled, Colt could feel it rattling in his bones. It made it feel like the sky was about to crack open at any moment. The dark water that waited below them was also ominous. The thought of willingly rowing out into it suddenly seemed like madness to Colt.

He could feel the nervousness among them like a sixth person. Before it had a chance to truly set in, he took Nyoko by the hand and led her towards the area where they had readied the lifeboat earlier in the day.

"How long do you think it's been like this?" Anne yelled to them over the wind.

"Not long," Heath said. "I didn't sleep well...I kept waking up off and on. I don't think we missed the start of it by any more than five or ten minutes."

What Colt thought, but didn't say, was: *In this case, five or ten minutes might make a huge difference.*

When they reached the lifeboat, Colt immediately realized that in the nervousness of waiting for the storm, they had all forgotten to discuss a very important detail. One of them would have to lower the boat into the water with the crank along the stack of other, unusable boats. He decided then and there that he would not allow it to become an issue.

"Get in," Colt said, guiding Nyoko into the boat.

As she climbed inside, clutching to her laptop case as always, she looked around the boat, saw the ropes, and then made the connection. "Hell no," she said. "Colt, how will you make it?"

"I'll jump," he said. "Easy."

"No way," Heath said. "I'll do it. I can—"

"This is non-negotiable and a waste of time," Colt said. "With a life jacket, I'll be fine."

"No," Heath said. "No life jacket." He reached into the lifeboat and pulled one of the life jackets from a small bundled pile along the front of the boat. "Remember…this ship is from the 30s. You hit the water from this height in one of these stupid things and you'll get whiplash."

He showed Colt the thin white vest that really looked like nothing more than cardboard covered with some weird sort of nylon to prove his point. Colt took it and nodded.

"The life ring," Nyoko said, pointing to the stern of the ship. Colt looked in that direction and saw two life rings hanging from the rails.

He nodded and raced off to grab one as the others hauled themselves into the lifeboat. By the time he got back, they were all in, Anne taking great care to slide up next to Tyler. Tyler was now clutching the rifle in his hands as if it was also a flotation device rather than a deadly weapon. Seeing him hold it in such a way made Colt a little uneasy.

As Colt grabbed the crank and started to turn it, thunder boomed again. As if triggered by the thunder, the wind seemed to pick up. The big ship creaked everywhere around them, showing signs of its age and neglect.

For a moment, Colt feared the crank was not going to move. It gave a bit at first, lowering the lifeboat by the ropes roughly a foot or so, but then the crank seemed to stick. He supposed it was rusted and tight with age. He pushed with all of his might and it only gave the briefest bit. It groaned in protest.

"Damn," he said.

He took a step back, raised his leg, and kicked the lever. It shot forward with speed and the boat went down fast. Colt reached for the lever so quickly that he almost fell down. Below him, he could hear Anne shouting out in fear and surprise. The lever struck his forearm hard, sending a flare of pain through his arm. Pins and needles filled his hand as he grabbed the lever again. He peered over the side and saw that the free fall had dropped the boat another five feet or so.

"Everyone okay?" he yelled down.

"Just keep going," Heath yelled back up.

With the resistance in the crank gone, Colt was able to reel the boat down much faster. He kept peering over the side, and although he knew he was taking the boat down as fast as it would go, it seemed to be taking forever. And all the while, the storm was raging beside them, blowing minutes of their already questionable time away.

Finally, the lifeboat touched the water. Colt fumbled with the ropes along the davit, finally untethering the lifeboat's ropes. With that done, there was only one thing left for him to do. He grabbed the flimsy-looking life ring and climbed up on the rails next to the davit. He saw the lifeboat down there and watched as everyone on board moved around to allow more room for the two oars that Heath and Tyler were now plunging into the water, pushing the boat away from the *Princess Celeste.*

Colt tried not to think about how far he had to jump. How far was it down there to the black water? Thirty feet? Forty?

Keep trying to fool yourself, he thought. *It's probably more like fifty.*

"Ah the hell with it," he muttered.

He climbed up to the top of the rail and looked down one more time. He slid over to the left, making sure he wouldn't strike the lifeboat when he jumped. When he was certain he was in the best position possible, he let go of the rail and hugged the life ring tight to his chest. He took one last step up, planting both feet on top of the rail.

Then he jumped.

On the way down, time seemed to stop, and his falling seemed to make the darting rain feel like little knives pricking at his skin.

He had just enough time to wonder if he was ever going to hit the water and then he did.

The breath went whooshing out of him, and the last thing he thought before he went under, was that it felt like hitting concrete rather than water.

The life ring went flying from his hands, and the world was swallowed up by an ocean that existed hundreds of millions of years ago.

SEVENTEEN

The world was all noise and chaotic motion. There was a tightness in his chest that he thought was the feeling of death rushing in and taking him. But then he felt something familiar sweeping through his body, a relief that seemed to make the tightening in his chest go away. A pleasant sort of burn raced through him and then, in a rush of heat, something seemed to radiate through him.

Breathing. He was breathing and it hurt, but it was a wonderful pain.

He was barely aware of being pulled over something slick and then he felt hands on him. There was only darkness, although he sensed that his eyes were open. He then felt something in the midst of the breathing, realizing that his airways were clogged. He felt something surging up through his body and then he coughed.

Saltwater came spewing out of his mouth, and it was this bitter taste that seemed to bring him around and clue him into what was going on.

"Colt?" someone was screaming. "Colt?"

"Yeah," he said through a croaking sort of gag.

He felt a set of arms wrap around him and realized that his entire body felt limp. He remembered jumping from the rail of the *Princes Celeste* and striking the water hard. After that, there was nothing.

How long was I under?

The thought was scary and it raced through his mind like a storm of sleet. He fell against the arms that were still wrapped around him, and when his vision finally decided to return, he saw Nyoko. She looked worried and even a bit scared—something that he was not accustomed to seeing from her. That, more than anything else, brought him around.

He gasped and rolled over onto his back, drawing in air. He saw the others that had dared this reckless escape looking down to him. Above them, he saw the black sky, the storm coming in and making the night seem all the more menacing. He saw flickers of lightning up there and heard the low, consistent rumble of thunder.

"Are you okay?" Nyoko asked.

"Yeah," he said. "How long was I under water?"

"Maybe a minute and a half," she said. "It was plain dumb luck that Heath was able to pull you over. That little life ring caught on the crook of your elbow and brought you up. You're lucky as hell to be alive."

He nodded, finding this easy to believe. Slowly, he managed to get to his knees, leaning against the side of the lifeboat. Heath was on one side with an oar in the water and Tyler was on the other side. Nyoko and Anne sat in the rear of the boat, Anne looking like she was extremely close to slipping into some sort of fugue. One thing was for sure: if they made it out of this alive, she was probably never going to be the same woman she had been before getting lost in the Triangle.

Fairly quickly, Colt saw that the storm was actually working *for* them. The wind was pushing at their backs, creating waves that pushed them farther away from the *Princess Celeste*. As his breathing became more regular and he started to get some of his strength back, he wished there was another oar so he could help push them along.

The wind was picking up, and while it was still not causing any dangerous conditions on the water, Colt wasn't sure how much longer that would be the case. It howled around them, and the rain continued to fall in light patters that the wind seemed to put a bit of stinging force behind.

Colt looked ahead into the storm and again saw the odd form of horizontal lightning he had spotted for a moment as he had been pulled from the water. It danced in an odd pattern that clued him in to the fact that what he was seeing was not lightning at all.

"Are those our lights?" Colt asked, pointing towards them.

"I'm not sure," Heath said. "The storm is making it hard to tell. It sure as hell doesn't look like plain old lightning, though, huh?"

"No. it doesn't."

Colt then looked to the churning dark water all around them. He wondered just how difficult it would be to see another *Cryptoclidus* before it was too late. Or maybe it wouldn't be a *Cryptoclidus* this time. What if something much more menacing chose to come to the surface for a bit to check out all of the commotion the storm was causing?

Colt did his best to shut the thought out of his head. For now, until such a threat presented itself, they had enough problems to contend with—namely trying to reach those mysterious lights and hope they were the answer to getting back home.

For the first time in a very long time, Colt could only stand idly by while his fate was decided by other people and forces beyond his control. He stared out into the storm, and the endless contrast of black on black as the night and the sea merged into a black void on the horizon. He stared towards the flickering lights in the sky, racing back and forth like spastic bolts of energy, while the storm and the wave pushed their lifeboat along.

EIGHTEEN

Ten minutes later, the storm died down a bit. The wind came to a slow halt, and the thunder grew quiet. It was still there, only not as violent and pronounced. Colt had regained most of his composure by then but felt the strength he had regained start to shrink back away as he started to fear that the storm they hoped would carry them out of here had died out before it had even properly begun.

"I think we're okay," Nyoko said, looking up to the sky. She pointed to the north, where a much larger group of dark storm clouds were crawling towards them. "I think it's just a break in the storm."

Colt nodded, but looked ahead of them, towards the faint lights that seemed to hang there. They were growing dimmer and dimmer as the storm died out, and he had the distinct feeling that if they flared out altogether, they could be in some trouble. Without those lights, any hope of escaping was gone. He was becoming more and more certain that those lights were intrinsically linked to the highways of the Triangle he had mentioned when he, Nyoko, and Heath had been in their own little life raft. He was starting to think of those lights as an exit on an interstate highway. Right now, they were between exits, making a U-turn on a road they were unfamiliar with in the hopes of getting back on their original course.

And if those lights weren't there in the sky, they had no exit.

But before he had time to properly worry, the wind started to pick back up, and a huge boom of thunder rolled across the ocean. Colt felt the vibration of it in the wooden floor of the boat and was again reminded that this fragile little boat was all that separated them from the undiscovered prehistoric monsters that swam in the depths beneath them.

His attention was broken by the sounds of gagging from the back of the boat. He turned to see what was happening just in time to see Anne throwing up. She did her best to get to the side of the rowboat, but some of it ended up along the floor in the back of the boat.

"Is she okay?" Nyoko asked.

When Tyler looked at them, he appeared to be on the verge of tears. "Yeah," he said. "She's just really nervous."

"That makes two of us," Colt said.

"Hell," Heath said. "I think that makes *all* of us."

Colt waddled to the back of the boat and held his hand out to Tyler. "Let me handle some of the rowing."

"I'm good," Tyler said. "You nearly drowned a little while ago, man."

"I'm fine. Give me the oar and take care of your wife."

Tyler gauged him for just a moment before handing over the oar. Colt took the oar and took position on the opposite side of the boat from Heath. It took him a few strokes, but he eventually fell into sync with him. Pushing against the sea as it rushed behind them, pushing them forward, felt deceptively easy. Colt tried not to let himself get too comfortable, though. If the wind picked up significantly, it would only take one of the waves that was currently ushering them along to swell up behind them and knock their little boat over.

Colt looked behind them and saw that they were further away from the *Princes Celeste* than he had hoped. She was still back there, but there was easily one hundred yards between their boat and the ship. It looked like a 3-D smudge against the night, almost like some huge chunk of abstract rock that had come bursting through the ocean floor.

"Colt?"

Heath's voice tore his gaze away from the *Princess Celeste*. Colt turned at the sound of his name and saw that Heath was staring out to sea. His gaze was aimed to the left, a bit further out.

Colt looked in that direction and saw nothing at first. But then after a few seconds, he saw the lump-like shapes darting back and forth among the white caps of the waves. The shapes were hard to make out, but he knew it was long, and that it was breaching the surface only to go under moments later. Whatever he was seeing there, seemed to be several of them, darting up and over the water in a manner that was very much like dolphins.

"Any idea what those are?" Heath asked.

"I can't see well enough to make them out," Colt said. "Nyoko?"

"If I had to guess, it might be some form of a *Plotosaurus*. But I didn't think they could swim so fast."

"Are they dangerous to us?" Tyler asked from the back.

"In this ocean, during this storm," Nyoko said, "I think just about anything could potentially be dangerous for us."

The one relief Colt felt in seeing them was that they seemed to be heading further away from them. He wondered if they were spooked by the storm or drawn to it. The way they were swimming made it appear as if they were drawn to it, enjoying a nighttime swim in the chaos.

Colt kept his eyes on them, but kept paddling. When he could no longer see their murky shapes, he looked ahead of them. The flickering lights were certainly brighter now, as if they were responding to the strength of the storm. Now, they no longer resembled lightning; instead, it was almost like seeing a completely white version of the Aurora Borealis. While he obviously had no way to know for sure, he was almost certain whatever the source of those lights might be, they were their ticket out of here. It was almost like instinct—something he felt way down in his guts.

What he did not feel particularly certain about, though, was whether or not they would make it to those lights before the storm came to an end.

But he couldn't think like that. He had to keep focused and—

His hopeful thoughts were dashed when something enormous breached the surface of the water and splashed back down less than twenty feet away.

In the back of the boat, Anne screamed.

"What was that?" Colt asked, looking to Nyoko.

"I didn't see it," she said. "But it had to have been a—"

Beside them, the thing rose up again. It was extremely close now, so close that as it came up out of the water, Colt could feel the boat shifting. His knees locked up, and he held the oar dumbly in his hands.

He looked to the right, where the huge shape remained above the surface, staring at him with a huge reptilian eye that looked almost impossibly sinister against the backdrop of the storm.

NINETEEN

Anne's screams were now louder than the wind (which, even now, continued to grow in tenacity and volume), and Colt had a terrifying moment where he badly wanted to reach around and smack her with the oar. Instead, he craned his neck, still looking at the impossibly huge head that stared at them from less than ten feet away, and whispered to the back of the boat.

"Tyler, could you please try to get her to calm down?"

He heard Tyler murmuring to her, yet his own voice was laced with fear. As for Colt, he was scared but not too badly. After all, the eyes that were regarding them from the water were similar to the eyes that had spied on them as they had climbed aboard the *Princess Celeste* earlier in the day.

It was another *Cryptoclidus*—maybe even the very same one they'd encountered earlier—and it did not appear to have any real malicious intent. It was just *there*, sort of checking things out. It made a noticeable chuffing noise as it remained there and then turned its head left and right. Its grey and rather bulbous head was a wonder in and of itself, making Colt surprisingly calm. There was something nearly mystical about the creature, something majestic and peaceful.

Still, its size was beyond intimidating.

"This is amazing," Nyoko said.

It was, but Colt could not find the nerve to utter an agreement. He watched the *Cryptoclidus* for a bit longer, and after what felt like an hour (but was surely no longer than thirty seconds or so), the creature slowly lowered its head back down beneath the water and disappeared.

The lifeboat was dead silent for several seconds. Anne's screams had stopped at Tyler's assistance, although she was breathing heavily as a result of her panic. The wind rocked them slightly, and the rain pattered down almost musically.

Colt found that he was slightly afraid to put his oar back into the water. While the *Cryptoclidus* might be completely harmless, the idea of it surfacing directly beneath them and destroying the lifeboat was one that was too easy to envision. He looked to Heath, also a little hesitant to put his oar back into the water from the looks of it, and they both nodded to one another. Slowly and with great caution, they both started to row again. Colt looked back up to that white flickering in the stormy sky, using them as his guide.

"This was a mistake," Anne said softly from the back.

"A mistake?" Heath asked.

"Yes," she said. "We should have never left the ship. It was stupid."

"Anne…" Tyler said, but stopped there.

"We have to go back," she said. "Quickly, please. We have to go back. We have to get out of the water and away from those monsters…"

She was pleading with them, her voice on the brink of hysteria. Tyler still looked as if he might start weeping at any moment. He sat firmly with his arm around his wife, looking just as helpless as she was.

"If we go back," Colt said, "we'll starve soon enough. It's out a question. If we go back, we die eventually."

"You don't think I know that?" Anne shouted. "You don't think Tyler and I discussed that several times a day? But at least starving is something we can handle, something we can accept. Being out here with these *things* is madness."

No one said anything to this. Colt and Heath continued to row. Nyoko was looking in all directions methodically like a guard on duty, trying to keep an eye out for the next potential threat. In the back, Tyler still held Anne tightly. She started to cry softly as she realized that her pleading was doing no good.

For a moment, Colt felt quite bad. The Gellers had been here on their own, dealing with their imminent death and meager hopes of escape in their own way. And then along came these complete strangers, offering them scant solutions. And now, here they were, all together in a lifeboat in the middle of a raging prehistoric sea because those strangers had assured them that they had the answers.

Colt was torn out of his reverie by the sound of another splash. At first, he thought it was just the surge of water against the boat. The storm, while not really growing any stronger, continued to swell around them. But out of the corner of his eye, he saw motion—a familiar movement that was extremely close to the boat.

"I think it might be more *Plotosauruses*," Nyoko said, noticing that he was startled.

He turned to his right and saw another break the surface, followed by two more. They were coming to the surface and curving directly back under. They closest one was no more than five feet away, splashing water into the boat. As it went under, they all felt a thump against the front end of the boat.

Heath drew up his oar right away, as if he had been shocked. "The damn thing hit my oar," he said. "I think it—"

The boat shook then, the wood splintering along the left side along the top. The boat pitched slightly to the left and as it did, a *Plotosaurus* came leaping from the water. Colt was again reminded of a dolphin, but this thing was easily twice the size of the biggest dolphin Colt could imagine. It moved fast and he could not get a clear view of it. He did see a wedged fin shape darting under the water.

He saw Tyler in the back of the boat, angling to the edge and raising his rifle. He wasn't sure if shooting the beasts was going to do any good and, more than that, he also wondered if it might cause more problems.

"Heath," he whispered. "Keep rowing."

"What if that thing hits us again?" he asked.

"Then we're screwed," Colt said. "But we're also screwed if we stay here." To motivate Heath, Colt started rowing on his own. After a few strokes, Heath did the same.

After three strokes forward, Tyler started firing the rifle.

The sounds were almost puny in the midst of the storm and the frantic sea, but they were still alarming. Everyone in the boat wheeled around to see what exactly was happening. Even Anne had jumped up and shied away from her husband as he leaned over the right side of the boat, firing rounds into the water.

Much to Colt's dismay, he saw a *Plotosaurus* by the side of the boat. It was submerging back under the water, but it was doing so very slowly. Even in the darkness of night and the motion of the sea, Colt could see the murky red tendrils of blood as it sank down. Colt was pretty sure he's heard three shots so far. If all three had landed, he supposed it could have seriously injured the *Plotosaurus*.

Working on nerves that felt nearly fried, Colt dropped the oar and went for the rifle. Tyler saw him coming but reacted too slowly. Colt grabbed the gun and yanked hard at it. It came easily, as Tyler's grip was slick with sea and rainwater.

"What the hell are you doing?" Colt asked.

"That damn thing was trying to sink us!"

"Maybe," Colt said. "But now it's in the water, bleeding. We've already seen two different kinds of dinosaurs in less than an hour.

All of that free-floating blood has the potential to attract some *really* nasty ones."

Tyler suddenly looked very afraid. He peered over the side of the boat like a man in a dream, making Colt wonder if he, too, was going to go the way of his wife. Anne, meanwhile, sat slumped in the back of the boat, staring at nothing in particular. The evidence of where she had been sick earlier still clung to the bottom of the boat directly by her feet.

"Sorry," Tyler said. The word came out almost like a little moan that was quickly overtaken by the noise of the wind.

"It's okay," Colt said. "We're all a little out of sorts here."

Having no better idea, he handed the rifle over to Nyoko. She took it, but gave it a distrusting look. Colt knew that if she had to make the decision between protecting her laptop or protecting the rifle, the rifle might possibly end up at the bottom of the ocean.

Colt and Heath continued to row onward. Overhead and slightly in front of them, the white lights in the sky remained constant, swirling and flickering like phantoms. Colt looked behind them and could barely see the *Princess Celeste* anymore. He thought he could just barely make out the shrinking shape of it, but it was mostly lost in the darkness.

"I'm sorry," Tyler said again.

Colt looked back to tell him not to worry about it but realized that Tyler was no longer talking to him. The last *I'm sorry* had been directed at Anne. He was now sitting with his wife, holding her to him and rocking steadily. His face was buried in her hair as he apologized over and over again.

Colt wasn't sure exactly what Tyler was apologizing for, and he also knew that it was none of his business. So he turned back around and kept paddling with his eyes set on those phantom lights that he hoped would lead them home.

TWENTY

Roughly twenty minutes after Tyler had shot the *Plotosaurus*, Colt started to feel a bit of pressure to the air. It was hard to explain at first, but as it grew, it reminded him of taking off in an airplane. The pressure he was feeling was similar to the moment in an airplane just before your ears popped from the change in altitude.

He looked over to Nyoko and just as he was about to ask if she felt anything different, she nodded and said, "You feel that, too?"

"Same here," Heath said.

"What is it?" Tyler asked from the back of the boat. He and Anne were still huddled tightly together, but they both seemed to be more present now.

"A pressure change, I'd guess," Colt said.

"I felt something very similar to it both times before I went into the lights in the Triangle," Heath said.

Anne looked up to the sky, her eyes hopeful for the first time since they had gotten into the lifeboat. "Is it working? Are we almost there?"

No one answered her because it was actually quite hard to judge the distance between their little lifeboat and the lights. While they had certainly appeared to grow larger as they had approached, they still looked far away. Still, the change in the atmosphere was undeniable and surely indicated that *something* was different here.

Just as he had grown accustomed to the pressure, the wind started to increase. It was still at their backs, and he could feel the force of it pressing against the boat and his arms as he continued to row. Thunder boomed overhead, massive guttural noises now. Each time it tore across the sky, Anne let out a little shriek in the back of the boat. And all the while, the phantom-like white light overhead remained constant and, Colt thought, were maybe even growing a bit brighter.

Colt felt his ears pop, and this was followed by a slight headache. As this settled in, the lifeboat caught a huge surge from the wind. It was pushed forward and struck a nearby wave at an angle. The entire boat sliced to the left, the back end going nearly horizontal. Anne screamed, and Tyler wrapped her tightly into his arms, locking his hands around her waist. The boat came over the wave and settled in a valley between several other large waves, bobbing chaotically as Colt and Heath continued to row forward as much as the storm would allow.

Even though the surging water was behind them, pushing them forward, it was still incredibly hard to row. The ocean had a mind of its own and seemed to be fighting against the initial push of the wind. More than that, Colt noticed that a new wind had picked up, and this one was coming from the east. Rowing against this new wind was brutal, and he didn't know how much longer he'd be able to do it.

The white lights in the sky now seemed to have grown small tendrils that flashed out in forks, almost like the streaks of lightning they had first seen when stepping out onto the deck of the *Princess Celeste.* Soon after that, Colt started to feel a new sensation in the air; the hair on his arms started to stand on end and then relax only to prick back up again. The pressure change was still there as well, and it all combined to create a very anxious feeling within the boat. Whatever was going on around them, Colt could not feel it in his guts as well as in his head.

"We're heading into an electrical storm," Nyoko called out, looking up to the evert-shifting white lights.

"This has to be it then, right?" Heath asked.

Colt saw that Heath was also exhausted, his arms slouched as he still continued to place the oars into the water. Colt that that this *was* it but didn't dare vocalize such a thing. He simply continued to paddle forward, his shoulders aching and his lungs burning.

"Hey…guys?"

It was Anne's voice, speaking up meagerly from the back. Colt looked back to her and saw that she was pale, but her eyes were wide with that looked to be wonder.

"Yeah?" Colt asked.

"What's that?"

She pointed ahead and to the left. Everyone looked in that direction and they all saw it at once. A light had appeared, as thin as a crack in a wall, but it blared with light just as white and intense as the lights in the sky. It was hard to tell for certain among the violence of the storm, but Colt was pretty sure it was moving, swaying like the lights above.

"That," Colt said, "is our way out of here."

The splinter of white light was about yards away. In the midst of the night and the still-growing storm, it was almost like a lighthouse in the distance, calling them to land.

Colt and Heath shared a knowing look and seemed to sigh simultaneously. Worn out and tired, they still plunged the oars into the water. They worked hard to redirect the boat so that it would angle over towards the seam of light that seemed to hover over the water. The waves and wind made it incredibly hard, and by the time they had gained any traction, both men were crying out in frustration from the effort of it all.

When the boat was directed towards the light, Tyler lunged forward and offered to take the oar from Colt. He gave it over with some hesitation, but was pleased to see that Tyler seemed more determined than ever. He plunged the oar in and went at it with strength bred out of the desire to live. On the other side, Nyoko took Heath's oar, and with that, the lifeboat was headed straight ahead with fresh power at the oars. They were moving much slower as they had to now fight against the water rather than pushing along with it, but they were still moving slightly forward towards the light.

No one in the boat said a word. They were all frozen in anticipation. Colt didn't dare set *all* of his hopes on those light out of fear that they'd reach them and nothing would happen. Still, he seemed to know. The lights above and the light ahead of them were very much the same as the ones they had seen in the plane with Heath earlier in the day.

With his eyes on the crack of light—which seemed to be growing wider by the moment—Colt then noticed the ripples in the air for the first time. They shimmered like heat from the pavement on a brutally hot day, slipping bits of color into the night: purple, yellow and a clear sort of white. They darted here and there, spiraling outward in thin trails and then disappearing only to be followed by others.

"You guys see that?" Colt asked.

Nyoko could only nod, her mouth slightly agape. She said nothing, but Colt knew what her scientific mind was thinking. Those ripples were roughly the same sort of thing science fiction movies had taught the world distortions of space might look like. In particular, scenes from *Contact* and *Interstellar* popped up in Colt's mind.

He almost spoke this thought aloud but was cut off before he could begin. A rumble of thunder boomed nearby with such veracity that the lifeboat trembled. He had to catch on to the side of the boat to keep from falling and—

When he was splashed from head to toe with water, he realized that the noise he'd heard wasn't thunder. It had been the sound of something massive erupting from the ocean. He wheeled around to his left and saw that Heath was frozen in terror, looking up at a hulking shape that was falling back into the water.

As soon as it hit the water, the boat rocked violently again. Colt looked at the water and could clearly see the back of something, barely breaching the surface.

He tried to understand the massive size of the thing but the dark water made it impossible. All he knew for sure was that whatever it was, it was swimming in an arc and circling back towards them.

It was coming with ferocious speed, headed directly for their boat.

TWENTY-ONE

Anne was screaming again, but Colt was barely aware of it. All he could hear was the wind, the thunder, and the growing sound of the water splashing up in front of them as the monstrosity that had jumped up moments ago came rushing at them. The world was all noise and blackness as it barreled towards the boat.

At the last moment, the beast seemed to change its mind and veer off a bit. Still, this change in direction did not spare the lifeboat. The massive body crashed into the left side, causing the boat to split down the side. The entire lifeboat shuddered and pitched forward a bit, sending everyone stumbling backwards. In the back of the boat, Tyler stumbled over Anne as they both tried to stay on their feet. Colt didn't see exactly how it happened, but their legs tangled up and when Tyler went falling, he lost his balance as the boat pitched forward. They all watched helplessly as he went over the side.

Anne's cry of shock broke through the storm and seemed to unfreeze everyone else within the boat. Colt raced to the left side of the boat to help Tyler and saw two things at once that made him realize there was a very good chance that he would die very soon.

First, the crack along the side of the boat went all the way to the bottom, sketching across the floor a few inches from his feet. The crack was about three inches wide, and the boat was already taking on water.

The second was that the massive monster that had come charging at them was currently racing back up through the water.

He saw it coming with ferocious speed, its black mass just dark enough to be seen through the almost equally black sea.

He opened his voice to scream a warning but did not have time. The beast came rocketing out of the water, rocking the boat backwards and several feet out of the water. Colt knew right away that they were going to be thrown from the boat so he reached for Nyoko as they went airborne. His hand barely missed her waist as they were tossed back, and in that final moment, just before the boat landed squarely on its right side in the water and threw all of them out, Colt got a complete glimpse of the monster.

It had a dark hide and a massive set of jaws that reminded Colt lightly of an alligator, only of an epic size. The creature was easily thirty feet long—maybe even forty, although it was hard to be certain as some of it remained underwater.

Colt saw a flash of the thing's massive teeth just as it snatched Tyler up out of the water and then Colt was also in the water. The waves rushed over his head and carried him on, still in the direction of the lights they were headed for. He quickly started swimming for the surface, the water cold but not stunningly so.

When his head surfaced, the world seemed to have been tilted. The swell of waves all around him and the dark sky overhead made it hard to get himself oriented. The only way he managed not to grow dizzy and disoriented was by keeping his eyes on the tottering shape of the boat several feet in front of him. As he set his eyes on the boat, he saw Anne Geller clinging to the back of it, screaming into the sea and storm for Tyler. Colt wondered if she had missed the sight of her husband being devoured by the monster and his heart went cold.

As Colt started swimming forward, something brushed by his leg under water, and he let out a scream. The same thing that brushed his leg then landed on his back and then broke the surface of the water to find his shoulder. He wheeled around defensively, trying to splash away, and saw Nyoko's face. She was gasping for air, her eyes wide with terror.

"Mosasaur," she said. "Colt…it's a mosasaur."

Overhead, thunder boomed again, and it drowned out the sound of Anne's screaming.

"What do we do?" Colt asked. His eyes were darting all around them, looking for any indication that the mosasaur was coming back. He figured it probably would if it had enjoyed the taste of Tyler Geller.

As Colt looked frantically around for any hope of safety, he saw Heath breach the surface of the water no too far away from the lifeboat. He blindly started swimming for it, apparently drawn by Anne's screams.

"I don't know," Nyoko said. "You?"

"I think the plan stays the same. We make it to those lights even if we have to swim. Although, I'd much rather try to push the boat back over."

She nodded, and they swam together towards the boat. Colt didn't think it felt like swimming, though. He was being pushed by the large waves, carried by the tremendous force of the sea. His legs and arms were moving in swimming motions, but it made him feel silly—it was ridiculous to think he had any real sway over which way he was carried.

As the waves pushed them towards the boat, Colt realized that the boat itself was also being carried. He saw that Heath had managed to reach the edge of it, clinging along to its upturned side. As Colt and Nyoko neared it, he could see the wooden plank seats and the old rickety floor. Sure, that floor had a crack in it that was taking on water, but even that would be preferable to floating in a dark ocean with a fabled mosasaur lurking in the darkness. The boat, for now, seemed caught in a valley between swells. If luck panned out for them, Colt was fairly certain that one more large wave from behind would push him and Nyoko directly towards it.

As it turned out, luck was with them. A wave picked them both up, high enough so that Colt could feel the rough wind at his back. The wave curled downward and dropped them, sending them under for a moment. As Colt went down, he grabbed Nyoko's hand. When they went under, the force of the water nearly pulled them apart, but he clamped down over her wrist with his free hand. When the surge of water over their heads rushed by, Colt started kicking for the surface and felt Nyoko coming along with him.

They surfaced at the same moment, and Colt was almost stupefied to see that the lifeboat was no more than ten feet from them, bobbing to the right and caught at the base of a gathering wave. Colt started swimming to it as quickly as he could and managed to draw Heath's attention.

"What the hell was that?" Heath shouted.

In his head, Colt was silently cursing both Heath and Anne, wishing they'd shut up. The screaming would only draw the damned thing back. He was pretty sure their screaming voices could be heard underwater, even over the storm…especially if the mosasaur was anywhere directly around them.

And Colt was pretty sure it hadn't gone far. Why would it when there was so much more easy food for it to pick up?

They finally reached the boat, and as they did, Colt caught sight of the mosasaur about thirty feet to the left. He could only see its back as it swam against the storm, but it seemed to be looping back, turning to come back towards them. It gave a sudden flick of its tail and went fully underwater, and that was somehow worse than actually being able to see it.

"We have to see if we can tip the boat back over," Colt told Heath.

Heath nodded, but his eyes were on the water, waiting for the mosasaur to show itself again. Anne, meanwhile, was still at the other end of the boat, clinging to it for dear life. Colt grabbed the edge of the lifeboat and pulled himself along until he reached Anne.

"Anne, we have to push the boat back upright, okay? You don't have to help, but you have to at least let go. Okay?"

She looked at him as if he was speaking a different language. She looked confused and was obviously in shock. "Tyler...where's Tyler?"

"I don't know," Colt lied. "But if we can get this boat back up, maybe we can find him. What do you say?"

It occurred to him then that if the mosasaur hadn't attacked them yet, it had passed by. Maybe it was curious about the new creatures in its territory. Maybe it was proceeding with caution or simply playing with its prey before devouring them. He did his best to not look around for it, because it would only distract him. All he was worried with in that moment was getting the boat back into place and making it to the fissure of white light that seemed to have cracked the sky twenty or so yards ahead of them.

He looked to that light and saw that the tendrils of its forks and branches had grown, taking on a sort of smudged appearance at their edges where it glowed. It looked inviting and sinister at the same time.

"Anne, can you help?" he asked.

She nodded and slowly repositioned herself to get a better grip on the right side, which was currently in the water. With the four of them all aligned along the side, they gave a heave that barely pushed the boat up at all. With the wind, the raging water, and their state of panic and exhaustion, it was much harder to move the boat than Colt had anticipated. Still, they managed to get it up...and not a moment too soon.

Behind them, a massive splash drew their attention. They all looked back at the same time and saw that it was the mosasaur, breaking the surface and again barreling straight for them.

Colt saw his death coming directly for him as he tried pulling himself into the boat. But even then, he knew it was a ridiculous thing to be doing. The mosasaur would tear into the boat, shattering into splinters. The last time, it had swerved away at the last moment, only causing minimal damage. But this time, Colt didn't think they'd be so fortunate.

As he came to this realization, he saw that Heath had already made it into the lifeboat. He was graciously reaching a hand out for Nyoko, which she was trying to take.

Acting on pure instinct, Colt grabbed Nyoko by the waist and pulled her hard to the side, away from the lifeboat. She screamed out in protest, but it was cut off as a rushing wave came by and splashed over their heads. Colt kicked away, bringing them both back up to the surface just as the mosasaur collided with the boat.

The results were catastrophic. The lifeboat was reduced to a few fragmented boards, splinters and dust. Anne went cartwheeling backwards out to sea, pitched into a wave where she disappeared for a moment. Heath was struck by the mosasaur's back as it tore through the boat, and he went flying to the left, directly towards the sliver of white light in the sky.

As Colt took all of this in, he also saw the mosasaur shift hard to the right. Colt watched it go and had no time to yell a warning.

Heath saw it at the last possible moment. Colt saw the instant where Heath realized what was happening but then all Colt could see was the massive back of the mosasaur. Heath was able to get out a single short scream, but it was cut off abruptly. The mosasaur moved slowly as it engulfed Heath and then seemed to rocket off towards the bottom of the ocean.

"Thanks," Nyoko said against this neck as she clung to him. He tried to keep her up but treading water with his tired limbs with her additional weight was too much.

"We have to swim," he said. "To the lights. Can you do it?"

She nodded, but he could tell that she had nearly admitted defeat already. "The lights," she said in a gasp, as if reminding herself of what they were doing.

"Come on," he said. "We can do this."

She let out a little whimper, and it broke his heart to see her in such a state. But he knew that he had to lead her now. He swam slowly alongside her, keeping her pace, knowing that at any moment the mosasaur could come back for a third helping.

Anne saw them swimming and followed suit, although she was several yards to their left. She was in hysterics now but was somehow finding the strength to push through. She was trying to say something, and as they drew closer, he thought it was Tyler's name over and over through a wrenching series of sobs.

Ahead of them the white crack in the sky looked amorphous now, no longer a crack but very similar to the swirling lights overhead. Colt looked up to them and saw that they almost looked to be alive. This was much different than viewing the phenomenon while in a plane, cruising by with great speed; witnessing it happen while mostly stationary as the Triangle did its magic in their presence was nearly awe-inspiring. It would have been magical as far as Colt was concerned if it weren't for the raging storm, the vicious sea, and the large prehistoric monster that was picking them off one by one.

Still, despite its beauty and obviously being out place, Colt knew that there was no certainty that it would provide them a way out. It was a good possibility, but there was also just as likely the possibility that it could cause them even more trouble.

But swimming through the dark ocean with a prehistoric beast somewhere beneath them, those odds seemed pretty damn good to Colt.

TWENTY-TWO

It was almost like swimming in water while knowing that there was a live electrical wire descending from the heavens. With each stroke towards the lights, Colt knew that there was a good chance that the mosasaur was coming up behind him or from directly beneath him. He knew he could die at any moment, but he also knew that they were close enough to those enigmatic lights that they could also do their trick at any moment as well.

That was, of course, assuming that whatever power the light shed would affect them down below in the water. The fear that this was all for not still lurked in the back of his head, almost as nagging as the threat of the mosasaur gulping him down at any moment.

Somewhere behind him, he could hear Anne gasping for breath. He turned to find her, but all he could see were the rising and falling of black waves. Somewhere among them, he thought, the mosasaur could be speeding up towards them. His heart was surging with adrenaline, and his heart felt like it might beat out of his chest; he was balancing along a line where death was on one side and insanity was on the other…and he fought to stay on that line, a line that would hopefully get him to the white flickering lights that were tauntingly close.

Nyoko was still beside him, moving as little as she could and letting the waves carry her. She was tired and obviously terrified, and Colt was pretty sure she was letting the terror have control of her. He knew the feeling well—not too long ago, he'd experienced that same sort of paralyzing fear on the very island she had rescued him from.

It was in that moment that Colt realized that he *had* to get Nyoko out of here. He had to get her home…or die trying.

He summoned up reserves of strength that he didn't know he had, ignoring the pains and aches in his chest and shoulders. He reached out for her and drew her close. At his touch, she seemed to relax a bit. She looked at him with a hopeful expression, and it was almost like looking at someone else. Seeing her like that, Colt knew that if they *did* make it out of this alive, their relationship would be changed—for the better or for the worse, he wasn't quite sure.

As they drifted together, and he swam towards the still-growing light ahead, the sky let out a hellacious blast of thunder. It sounded like the world had cracked open and Colt could feel the reverberations of it in the water. As if ushered in by the thunder, the wind picked up and added even more force for Colt to swim against. This wind was not at their back as the original gusts had been, but seemed to come from the west and then whip around to the north.

Two minutes later, Colt felt the first real pangs of panic sink into him. The water was simply too much to fight against now. The waves were far too rough to fight against, and he was being carried against his will. The only relief he found was that he was still being pushed towards the lights, albeit slower than before. His lungs were burning from the exertion he was putting forth, and his arms felt like taffy as he did everything he could to help Nyoko along. He was also aware that he no longer heard Anne. He couldn't remember the last time he'd heard her cries. He looked around but still saw no trace of her. She'd either been taken by the ocean or devoured quietly by the lurking mosasaur.

Colt was so close to the lights now that he could see their white glow on his skin. The one above the water was now almost like a root system beneath a tree, the arms snaking off in all directions and tapering off into glowing points that eventually sank back into the night. They were so close, but he didn't know if he had the strength to make it to them.

"Colt?"

Nyoko's voice was soft, little more than a whisper.

"Yeah?"

She nodded to the left and the frown on her face—her bottom lip drooping and quivering—made Colt not want to look in that direction. But he knew he had to, even though he was fairly certain of what he would see.

It was the mosasaur. It was several yards behind them, slinking along through the water. It appeared as if the storm was slowing it down a bit. Perhaps, Colt thought, the thunder is making it a bit apprehensive.

"Just hold on," Colt said.

And she did. She clung to him in a way that made it harder for Colt to stroke forward. A wave came crashing down on them from the right side and sent him under the water. He held on to Nyoko and started kicking up right away. Nyoko weighed next to nothing, but being that he was already beyond exhausted, it was like swimming to the surface with a concrete block strapped to his chest.

When he managed to reach the surface, he gasped for breath. On his shoulder, Nyoko was coughing and spitting up ocean water. All around them, the ocean seemed to be coming alive, waves rising and falling in no real order or alignment. They were simply everywhere, like unformed peaks of mountains. Overhead, the white lights were still in the sky, as present as ever. They were shining down on them now, almost blinding.

Another wave assaulted them, this time from behind. He went under at once, taking in a mouthful of salty water, His lungs burned as he shut them down while he was submerged, and he once more found himself fighting for the surface. He had to loosen his grip on Nyoko in order to get there, but he kept her in his grasp as he once again managed to breach the surface.

When he did, he saw the mosasaur right away. They had somehow come up behind it. It was being tossed to and fro in the storm as well and seemed to be trapped within a swell of waves. It went underwater less than twenty feet from them and Colt nearly envied the damn thing. Because if *he* went under again, he wasn't sure he'd be able to come back up.

He managed to kick a bit ahead, riding the crest of a wave for several yards. His body felt so ragged that he half expected the violent winds to snatch him right out of the water and carry him further out to see like a piece of trash caught in the wind.

When he came off the wave's crest, he almost lost his hold on Nyoko. She slipped from the cradle between his arm and his left side, and he only caught her because her armpit hooked his arm as she slipped. He kicked his feet to stay afloat as he pulled her back up and even that small effort sent them briefly underwater.

Colt hauled her back up and then brought them both back to the surface. And when he did, he almost wished he hadn't.

A massive wave was rising behind them, easily the largest he'd seen so far. He started to kick away from it but stopped after one single stroke. It was useless. Even if he could manage to avoid being aught along its base, it would still pummel them down into the water.

"I'm sorry," Colt said to Nyoko. He gave her a brief embrace as the wave reached its apex and then came crashing down around them.

Cot closed his eyes and felt the rush of water all around them, the sound filling his ears and the impact driving him down into the black heart of the prehistoric sea.

TWENTY-THREE

Colt felt his body being pulled and pushed like a doll, as if different currents of the sea were fighting for possession of his body. Through it all, he held on to Nyoko in the slight hope that they'd either resurface or that the lights they had been chasing in the sky would somehow save them at the last moment.

He was being crushed down in such a way that he could no longer tell up from down or left from right. Even if he had the strength and will to swim upwards to the surface (which he suddenly realized he didn't), he wouldn't have known which way to go.

He felt Nyoko shuddering against him, and he wondered how long it would be before those shudders turned into jerks and spasms as her body ran out of oxygen.

That's when he saw the white glow beneath him. At first, he thought it was the darkness of the ocean and the disorientation playing tricks on him; surely he was just seeing the glow of the lights in the sky, blazing their light through the water.

But no...this light was too bright for that. This light was beneath him, deeper in the water. And by God, it was *close*.

Using those lights as a guide, Colt started swimming. He stroked downward with his free hand and kicked fiercely. Nyoko was like an anchor tied to him and slowing him down, but he'd be damned if he'd let her go now. He swam and felt his chest tightening. His head was starting to ache and a sharp pain started to build within his lungs.

Ten seconds, he thought. *Maybe twenty if I'm lucky. After that, I'll drown.*

So he kicked downward and after a meager two kicks he was rewarded with…well, *something.* He wasn't sure *what* was going on. All he knew was that the water surrounding him no longer felt fluid. He still had to fight through it to reach the lights, but there was not as much resistance.

He kept his eyes focused on those lights, and they slowly seemed to grow outwards towards him. The dark sea was no longer dark and the light his water-shrouded eyes were seeing almost made it seem like daylight under the water.

That's what allowed him to see the mosasaur so clearly.

It was coming straight for him, to his right. It had no interest in the strange lights that resided underwater—the exact same sort of light they had chased above. It had its sights on the two small creatures that had dared to invade its sea.

The spike of fear that rocketed through Colt seemed to rob him of the oxygen that remained in his body. At the exact moment his lungs seemed to implode from inside, he noticed that Nyoko was now motionless against him.

With darkness closing in on him, slowly obliterating the glow of the lights beneath him, Colt used the last bit of his energy to kick down towards the lights. It seemed to him that it was nearly touching his free arm, his fingertips flirting with it.

His air gave out. He instinctively opened his mouth, and a gasp of nothing came out as water surged into his throat. He gasped and choked, beginning to drown. In his frantic movement, he saw the mosasaur coming, opening its jaws and revealing the chasm within, no more than ten feet away.

Colt wasn't sure which would be the best way to die.

He closed his eyes and held Nyoko's body tight. He didn't know if the lack of oxygen would kill him before the mosasaur devoured him.

And in that darkness, he did not really care.

He waited and felt a surge of tight pain rush through his body just as he felt the movement of the water against him as the mosasaur bared down on him. He waited for death. Any second now...

But instead, he heard the sound of wind.

TWENTY-FOUR

When he heard the sound of wind, Colt opened his eyes. When he did, he noticed that the weight of the ocean was no longer all around him, pushing him down. He coughed wretchedly, bringing up thick salt water. When it came out of his mouth and nose, the burning sensation was beyond awful, but it was the sweetest sensation he'd ever felt.

Through the tears that came with the coughing, Colt still saw the water but it was splitting around him. He was in a tunnel of some kind, a tube of white light and what looked almost like grey smoke. Intertwined through all of that were think pink filaments that almost looked like veins running through tissue and muscle.

He still held Nyoko and as far as he could tell, he was still in a swimming position. It almost felt like he was flying, only he knew that he wasn't the one doing the moving. He was being moved instead.

He thought of the analogy he had used before, about how there was a hidden highway somewhere within the Triangle, complete with exit ramps. He was taking one of those exit ramps right now; he was almost certain of it.

"Nyoko," he said. "Do you see it?"

"Hunh," was all she said. She stirred against his shoulder the slightest bit, but that was enough reassurance for him.

He tried to understand where he might be, and it was too much to grasp. If Nyoko's theories were correct, he was presently suspended in some sort of wormhole. He was exiting outside of space and time. For that moment within the tunnel, he was ageless. Infinite.

But just as soon as delusions of immortality sprang up, he could see the end of the tunnel just ahead of him. He saw more water, an endless expanse of it. But there was no storm on the other end of the tunnel. In fact, the sky looked crystal clear, and the ocean was calm.

As he neared the opening, the sound of wind increased although he felt no wind. The light started to flicker and the pink lines of light started to fizzle out. He was coming to the end of the tunnel and while the prospect of once again being stranded at sea was terrifying, at least he had been spared from drowning.

For now, anyway.

"We're almost there," he said. "Nyoko, you have to see this…"

He realized that his voice was breaking up as the lights sped up. The words were echoing in nowhere and being filtered through whatever odd space-time filter currently held him. He smiled at the idea of it all and then, in a blinding white flash, he found himself falling.

The tunnel was gone and he was falling through the air. It wasn't too much of a fall, really. He'd hardly had time to realize what had happened before he slammed into the water. When he hit, he lost his grip on Nyoko and instantly started swimming in the direction her body had gone.

He was beyond relieved to feel the water churning as her body swam quickly to the surface. Colt did the same, kicking for the top, the memory of his near-drowning far too fresh in his mind.

As they both popped up at the surface, they joined hands and tread along the water. While it was nice to have his lungs back in working order, Colt found that his body was still just as exhausted as before.

"Look," Nyoko said. "Over there…"

Colt looked to where she was pointing and could not make sense of what his eyes were taking it at first. But when he was able to accept it, he actually chuckled at the sight.

There were shards of the lifeboat that the mosasaur had destroyed scattered in the water. One of the pieces was the front quarter or so of the boat. More than that, Anne Tyler was clinging to its side.

Colt and Nyoko swam to her, covering the distance of about fifty feet. By the time they reached the floating debris and Anne, Colt was spent. He grasped the edge of the boat remnant and relaxed against it. Nyoko joined alongside him and was gasping for breath when her hand fell on the edge.

Colt looked to Anne and saw that her eyes were glazed over. She was certainly breathing but was unresponsive. She was in some sort of shock, staring out to the sea and completely unaware that Colt and Nyoko had joined her.

"Anne," Colt said. "Anne, can you hear me?"

He got no response at all. Not even a blink. Slowly and cautiously, he reached out and gently took her face in his hands. He turned her head in his direction, and she gave no resistance. When he had her eyes looking at him, he met her blank gaze.

"Anne. Hey. It's Colt. Do you hear me? Do you see me?"

A flicker of recognition passed by the empty gaze, and after a few moments, she nodded.

"Are you okay?" Colt asked.

"No," she said, her voice no stronger than the sound of a sigh. "I can't make sense of it. I need Tyler. I need—"

"Do you remember how you got here?" Colt asked.

He was sure her own experience was much like the one he'd just lived through, but he wasn't asking because he was genuinely interested. He was asking in the hopes of breaking through her shock. Maybe if he could get her to start talking, she'd come around a little more.

"I was thrown from the lifeboat," she said, her eyes suddenly taking on a bit of life. "I was thrown into the water, and I started swimming for the lights right away. But then storm got worse, and the waves got bigger. I got caught up in one, and it kept me underwater for a long time. When I came back up, my head hit the side of this." She said this, tapping on the fragment of the boat they all held on to. She smiled and added, "And the wave had carried me right to that light that seemed to be reaching down towards the water. I made it to that light and then...I don't know. There was a tunnel...lights...and then I was here."

Colt wasn't sure where *here* was and wondered if he was being naïve to think that they had returned to their home-time. Could the mosasaur still be lurking somewhere beneath them? For that matter, even if they *had* returned home, has the mosasaur managed to also be taken by the vortex or time tunnel or whatever the hell had rescued him from sure death?

It was not a pleasant thought, and he simply could not allow his mind to go there. Instead, he focused on Nyoko, noticing that she seemed to be coming around. She was exhausted and obviously scared, but she also seemed to be growing more alert by the minute.

For a while, there was only the sound of the gentle waves around them. The soft rocking of the front of the boat they all clung to was almost hypnotic. For a moment, Colt felt like he was a baby being rocked to sleep by the eldest mother of all.

The silence was broken by Anne's voice, as desperate and sad as ever. "Where are we?" she asked.

"There's no way to know for sure," Nyoko said. "Without my laptop..."

She trailed off, and Colt could sense the disappointment in her voice. All of the data she had collected was gone. Every shred of evidence they had accumulated about this trip was in the bottom of an ocean that still churned in the past hundreds of millions of years ago. While Nyoko was obviously upset about this, it irritated Colt, too. After everything they had gone through—everything they had seen and endured—they'd have nothing to show for it.

That realization was still not as intimidating as the possibility that they were essentially still stranded at sea. Even if they had managed to return back to their time, they were still in need of being rescued.

Under the water, Colt felt Nyoko reach out with her right leg, intertwining it with his left. It seemed cheesy and almost like something love-struck middle-schoolers might do, but he understood the need for the contact. It was more than support; it was the knowledge that no matter what happened, they'd be going through it together.

Colt slowly scanned the horizon. There was nothing but water, speckled by the foamy white caps of the slow persistent waves.

Beside him, Anne started to weep. He looked over at her and saw that she had turned away from them, looking in the opposite direction. Between her sobs, he could hear her saying her husband's name: "Tyler…Tyler…"

Colt could do nothing to help. He simply clung to the fragile safety of the lifeboat's front end and bobbed endlessly in the water to the sound of Anne Geller's grief.

TWENTY-FIVE

At some point during that fugue-like time, Colt noticed Nyoko's watch. On the *Princess Celeste,* it had been useless, its small digital numbers having been reduced to flickering shapes. But now, it showed numbers, indicating that it was 11:05 a.m. As they floated there and grew weaker by the moment, Colt would occasionally look at the watch

"The tunnel," Colt said, his voice sudden and sharp in the silence. "Are we assuming the storm opens and closes it?"

"I don't know," Nyoko said. Her voice was sleepy-sounding. "If anything, I think the storm itself is a response to time shift...an atmospheric response, maybe."

"How so?" Colt asked. He hoped that keeping her mind going would keep her alert.

"If you think of a rubber band...and if the course of time runs along that rubber band, it can stretch when pulled. So imagine that rubber band pulled to the point of nearly snapping. I think once it gets to that point, actual time—the time we live in—sort of gets distorted. And the storm is an atmospheric reaction to the magnetic shifts, and God only knows what else is occurring. That's just a theory, though."

Anne had turned to them now, her eyes puffy from crying. "Are we back home, though? Are back in *our* time?"

"There's really no way to know," Nyoko said.

"However," Colt said, nodding to Nyoko's wrist, "your watch appears to be working again."

"I noticed that, too," she said. "I just didn't want to dwell on it because we still don't really know for sure."

They fell into silence again, and somehow Colt managed to fall into something akin to a doze. He felt his fingers slipping away from the edge of the wood and kept snapping awake. He then realized that he was growing very thirsty, and he tried to focus on that in an effort to stay alert. He glanced at Nyoko's watch and saw that it read 1:58 now. The day slowly slipped away from them as he grew more and more certain that they'd end up dying while stranded at sea anyway. The only difference was that there was now no prehistoric beast on their tails.

And even that wasn't a certainty.

Again and again, Colt nodded off, lulled into a near-sleep by the soothing motion of the sea.

When he first heard the strange muted sound of what sounded like a weird stuttering drumbeat, Nyoko's watch read 3:11.

He thought he was imagining at first; maybe he'd gotten too much water in his ears and it was beginning to affect his hearing. He nearly ignored the sound completely but then saw that Anne was beginning to look around with a terrified expression on her face.

"You hear it, too?" Colt asked

"Yes. What is it?"

"I don't know."

Nyoko spoke up and Colt was glad to hear that her voice was back to normal: strong, determined, and authoritative. "It sounds mechanical," she said.

Colt wasn't sure about that. What he *did* know was now that he heard it for sure, he could not *un*hear it.

"My God," Anne said, her eyes narrowing into slits. With a trembling hand, she pointed into the sky.

Colt followed the direction of her finger and saw something up there, something small and moving. It took him a while to figure out that what he saw was small, because it was very far away. But second by second, it grew larger as it got closer.

He saw the basic shape of it and suddenly, the almost drum-like noise he'd heard made sense. It was the sound of an approaching helicopter, the noise coming from the propellers as it got closer to them.

Anne started crying again, and Colt could not tell if it was from the joy of what would hopefully turn out to be a rescue or the sorrow of not having Tyler there with her. He looked from Anne to Nyoko and saw the barest curve of a small touch to her lips. It was extremely good to see, and for just a second or two, he did not feel exhausted and beaten.

The helicopter drew closer and closer, finally getting so close that Colt could see the sun's reflection glinting from the windshield. It started to descend, the stuttering beat of its blades like divine music now. As it dropped closer and closer to the water, Colt felt the wind from the propellers in his hair and against his face. It made the water choppy, shaking the fragment of the lifeboat a bit, but compared to the storm they had come out of hours ago (or millions of years ago, Colt guessed), it was nothing.

He grasped the edge of the shattered boat and made a solemn vow to himself: when he was pulled from the ocean, and they made it out of this alive, he was never going near the water ever again.

TWENTY-SIX

From what Colt had been able to put together, the scenario behind their rescue was surprisingly simple but, as far as he and Nyoko were concerned, a little creepy.

When the plane had not returned to the airfield, the owner had called the police. After a day or so, the call to the police had been escalated, as the owner stated that he could not get in touch with the plane. No contact and no connection via the radio had alarmed the owner, making him wonder if there had been a crash of some sort.

Once word had gotten out, a few of Nyoko's business partners had heard. They'd made a few calls, and soon the basic search and rescue mission was pushed to the very top of the ranks. The Coast Guard was eventually contacted and, in the end, it was a Coast Guard helicopter that had spotted them floating in the water roughly forty-five miles to the north of Puerto Rico.

That was the easy-to-believe part. However, the part that had rattled both Colt and Nyoko was the fact that the search and rescue—from the moment the owner of the rental had called the police to the moment Colt, Nyoko, and Anne were raised up into the helicopter—had taken five days.

On the morning after their rescue, Colt and Nyoko had laid in bed in a motel room in Miami, trying to make sense of it. They were both in agreement that the course of their entire trip should have taken no more that twenty-four hours, and that was pushing it. They had taken off from the airfield shortly after eight o'clock in the morning and had nearly been devoured by a mosasaur that same night.

"The time we spent in the tunnel, though," Colt said. "I wonder how much time that took away from us. It was only a few seconds to us, but in real time, there's no telling."

"So you think we're victims of missing time?" she asked.

"I do."

They said nothing else after that. Colt was asleep again five minutes later.

They had been rescued just before four in the afternoon. By 5:30, they were checked into a hospital. Colt and Nyoko had been cleared by midnight, but Anne Tyler had stayed behind due to some sort of traumatic emotional stress. As far as Colt could tell, she had not mentioned the *Princess Celeste* or any prehistoric beast trying to eat them. He guessed that she assumed everyone would think she was crazy. Besides that, in spite of all of the impossible details of her story, she was still too bogged down by the death of her husband to really even care too much about it.

He supposed she'd tell her story one day and become popular on paranormal websites and forums. She'd rule Reddit for a few days and might even end up as a special guest on a History Channel show. But in the end, he thought her time in the Triangle would scar her more than any of them could understand.

Colt and Nyoko had stopped at the first hotel they came to; they checked in just after 1:00 in the morning and slept the sleep of the dead. The only reason Colt woke up when he did the following morning was because his stomach was growling. He'd gone down to the continental breakfast in the lobby and brought back fruit and muffins. They ate it in silence and then ended up back in bed. It was the first time they had gotten into a bed so quickly without the immediate prospect of sex.

After discussing the possibility of missing time and falling asleep again, Colt did not open his eyes again until it was dark outside. When he sat up in bed, he found that his arms and shoulders felt like shredded chunks of meat and his legs felt like they'd been crushed by a truck. He wondered just how much time they'd spent out in the ocean, treading water and swimming for their lives.

"You okay?" Nyoko asked.

"Just sore. God…so sore."

"Me, too."

"You want to go back home tomorrow and try to make sense of all of this?" he asked. "Maybe try to get some of it written down?"

"Yeah. After I get a new laptop."

"Yeah. That sucks."

"I'm curious," she said, giving him a tired yet peaceful look. "How sore are you?"

"Very. Why?"

She pulled back the covers and revealed her naked body—a body that had been naked ever since last night, but they had both been too tired to do anything about.

"On second thought," Colt said. "I think I'm feeling much better."

***

They'd been unable to leave when they wanted. They were packed up by nine in the morning and had just made it to the elevators when a man came down the hall from the opposite end of the hotel.

"Excuse me," the man said. "Colt McKinnon? Nyoko Hisakawa."

"That's us," Colt said. "And you are…?"

"Thomas Barber. NSA."

"What do you want?" Nyoko spat.

"Mrs. Hisakawa, let's not make this hard. You know why we want to speak with you."

"You want to know what happened?" she asked.

"I do. And I've been sent to ask that you consider coming to D.C. to make a full report."

"What for?" Colt asked.

Barber seemed perplexed at first, as if he wasn't sure if they were trying to play dumb or were genuinely surprised. "The two of you go missing in the Bermuda Triangle, and we're expected to think it's a coincidence?"

"Why would you even care?" Colt asked.

"Because ever since your first...*adventure,* we've kept our eyes on you—especially since you started working for Mrs. Hisakawa's company. Tell me...how long were you gone?"

"One day," Colt said.

"In our time or Triangle time?"

Colt and Nyoko were quiet at first, but after a few seconds, Nyoko spoke softly. "Five days."

"So you're missing four days?" Barber asked.

They both nodded.

"There's also the matter of the third man that went out with you," Barber said. "Heath Francis. He didn't come back. You said he died in the crash but...well, I'd like to know the whole story."

"That's all there is to tell," Colt said, but he knew he didn't sound convincing.

"And let me ask you something else," Barber said. "Anne Geller...the woman that came back with you. How long had she been missing?"

"Two weeks," Nyoko answered.

Barber made a chuffing sort of laugh. "Okay," he said. "All the same, I think you might want to think about coming out to D.C. We have something of a pet project concerning the project. Are you familiar with a ship called the *Princess Celeste?* It's a staple of Triangle lore."

Colt felt as if he had been slapped in the face but tried to hide it. Apparently, it did not work because Barber made that chuffing noise again. He reached into his coat pocket and pulled out a business card which he deftly handed to Colt.

"I suggest you call us," he said.

"Or?" Colt asked.

Barber said nothing. He pressed the down button by the elevators and nodded to them. "I think I'll take the stairs."

With that, he walked away, leaving Colt and Nyoko alone.

"You ever work with the NSA?" Colt asked her.

"No. But my father had some dealings with him. They kept wanting to do business with him—a *you scratch my back, I'll scratch yours* sort of thing."

"Do you think they had people stationed in the belly of the *Princess Celeste?*" Colt asked.

"It's possible. I can check later. My laptop might be at the bottom of the ocean, but I remember some of the names I saw."

The elevator arrived, and they took it down to the lobby. While Nyoko checked out, Colt went to the other end of the counter where a bored-looking busboy was setting out the day's newspapers.

"Excuse me," Colt said. "Look, I don't have my phone on me, and I'd really like to check the basketball scores from last night. Would you allow me to use your cellphone or maybe a laptop or something?"

"Sure," the busboy said. He reached into his pocket, pulled out his phone, and handed it over to Colt.

"Thanks a ton," Colt said. "I'll just be two minutes."

"Take your time."

Colt, of course, had no interest in basketball scores. He opened the phone's web browser and typed "Anne Geller disappearance" in the search bar. He got a few results and they all spelled out the same story. Anne and Tyler Geller went out sailing, leaving from a small beach just to the north of Miami. No one has seen them ever since.

He read two articles and got nothing new out of them. They were very small articles without many details. But as he was about to close out of the second article and had the busboy back his phone, he saw the one detail that meant the most.

It was at the top of the story, before the story even began. It was the date the article was published: July 27th, 2006.

Two weeks my ass, Colt thought.

A chill passed through him, and when Nyoko approached him from behind, he jumped a little.

"Something wrong?" she asked.

Without saying a word, Colt handed the phone to Nyoko. Within thirty seconds, she looked away from the screen, her eyes wide. Slowly, Colt took the phone from her and gave it back to the busboy.

Colt and Nyoko left the hotel like two sleepwalkers, holding hands as they stepped out into a world that was four days ahead of them.

TWENTY-SEVEN

The storm had passed half an hour ago, but the damage had been done. The boat had been tipped over, the sail a ruined memory of the once-expensive rig. They had managed to stay afloat, but the boat was sinking. Their only hope was to make it to the huge ship that seemed to be sitting still in the middle of the ocean.

"It doesn't look right," the woman said.

"It's either climb aboard that thing or sink with this boat," the man said.

"But it...I don't know. It looks *deserted.*"

The man looked hard ahead and thought that she was right. "We don't have a choice," he said. "But look...just in case, I packed everything we have." He patted the little knapsack and the two book bags he had brought out from the massively drenched cabin beneath them.

They floated on, nearing the boat and with every minute that passed, the man became more and more convinced that the ship *was* deserted. They were close enough now to see the name along the side.

"Look at that, Anne," he said. "That sounds familiar, doesn't it?"

"*Princess Celeste,*" Anne said. "I don't know."

She was too scared to really care, though. He knew that, and it terrified him more than anything else.

"Tyler, I'm scared."

"I know," he said. "I am, too. But we'll be okay. There *has* to be someone on that ship."

But even as he said that, he wasn't so sure.

Anne and Tyler Geller floated closet to the *Princess Celeste,* as if it were pulling them forward, a magnet for their fear. While neither of them knew it, this was not the first time they had approached the *Princess Celeste.* They had done it countless times before, climbing on board, spending several weeks and then forgetting it all only to open their eyes on their sailboat, two days into their anniversary trip out to sea.

As always, they drew so close to the ship that they could see the ladder along the back, the ladder they would use to climb aboard.

And every time, as Tyler Geller climbed that ladder, he thought he caught a glimpse of something in the distance, something with an impossibly long neck and a large head, peering out of the water—something that looked like a dinosaur.

But that was ridiculous. It was surely just his panicked and flustered mind playing tricks on him. He ignored it each time and climbed the ladder, having no idea that his life was now an infinite loop and that he would climb that ladder on the *Princess Celeste* again and again until the end of time.

CHECK OUT OTHER GREAT DEEP SEA THRILLERS

THEY RISE
by Hunter Shea

Some call them ghost sharks, the oldest and strangest looking creatures in the sea.

Marine biologist Brad Whitley has studied chimaera fish all his life. He thought he knew everything about them. He was wrong. Warming ocean temperatures free legions of prehistoric chimaera fish from their methane ice suspended animation. Now, in a corner of the Bermuda Triangle, the ocean waters run red. The 400 million year old massive killing machines know no mercy, destroying everything in their path. It will take Whitley, his climatologist ex-wife and the entire US Navy to stop them in the bloodiest battle ever seen on the high seas.

SERPENTINE
by Barry Napier

Clarkton Lake is a picturesque vacation spot located in rural Virginia, great for fishing, skiing, and wasting summer days away.

But this summer, something is different. When butchered bodies are discovered in the water and along the muddy banks of Clarkton Lake, what starts out as a typical summer on the lake quickly turns into a nightmare.

This summer, something new lives in the lake...something that was born in the darkest depths of the ocean and accidentally brought to these typically peaceful waters.

It's getting bigger, it's getting smarter...and it's always hungry.

CHECK OUT OTHER GREAT DEEP SEA THRILLERS

SEA RAPTOR
by John J. Rust

From terrorist hunter to monster hunter! Jack Rastun was a decorated U.S. Army Ranger, until an unfortunate incident forced him out of the service. He is soon hired by the Foundation for Undocumented Biological Investigation and given a new mission, to search for cryptids, creatures whose existence has not been proven by mainstream science. Teaming up with the daring and beautiful wildlife photographer Karen Thatcher, they must stop a sea monster's deadly rampage along the Jersey Shore. But that's not the only danger Rastun faces. A group of murderous animal smugglers also want the creature. Rastun must utilize every skill learned from years of fighting, otherwise, his first mission for the FUBI might very well be his last.

OCEAN'S HAMMER
by D.J. Goodman

Something strange is happening in the Sea of Cortez. Whales are beaching for no apparent reason and the local hammerhead shark population, previously believed to be fished to extinction, has suddenly reappeared. Marine biologists Maria Quintero and Kevin Hoyt have come to investigate with a television producer in tow, hoping to get footage that will land them a reality TV show. The plan is to have a stand-off against a notorious illegal shark-fishing captain and then go home.

Things are not going according to plan.

There is something new in the waters of the Sea of Cortez. Something smart. Something huge. Something that has its own plans for Quintero and Hoyt.

CHECK OUT OTHER GREAT DEEP SEA THRILLERS

MEGATOOTH
by Viktor Zarkov

When the death rate of sperm whales rises dramatically, a well-respected environmental activist puts together a ragtag team to hit the high seas to investigate the matter. They suspect that the deaths are due to poachers and they are all driven by a need for justice.

Elsewhere, an experimental government vessel is enhancing deep sea mining equipment. They see one of these dead whales up close and personal...and are fairly certain that it wasn't poachers that killed it.

Both of these teams are about to discover that poachers are the least of their worries. There is something hunting the whales...

Something big
Something prehistoric.
Something terrifying.
MEGATOOTH!

BLOOD CRUISE
by Jake Bible

Ben Clow's plans are set. Drop off kids, pick up girlfriend, head to the marina, and hop on best friend's cruiser for a weekend of fun at sea. But Ben's happy plans are about to be changed by a tentacled horror that lurks beneath the waves.

International crime lords! Deep cover black ops agents! A ravenous, bloodsucking monster! A storm of evil and danger conspire to turn Ben Clow's vacation from a fun ocean getaway into a nightmare of a Blood Cruise!

CHECK OUT OTHER GREAT DINOSAUR THRILLERS

JURASSIC ISLAND
by Viktor Zarkov

Guided by satellite photos and modern technology a ragtag group of survivalists and scientists travel to an uncharted island in the remote South Indian Ocean. Things go to hell in a hurry once the team reaches the island and the massive megalodon that attacked their boats is only the beginning of their desperate fight for survival.

Nothing could have prepared billionaire explorer Joseph Thornton and washed up archaeologist Christopher "Colt" McKinnon for the terrifying prehistoric creatures that wait for them on JURASSIC ISLAND!

K-REX
by L.Z. Hunter

Deep within the Congo jungle, Circuitz Mining employs mercenaries as security for its Coltan mining site. Armed with assault rifles and decades of experience, nothing should go wrong. However, the dangers within the jungle stretch beyond venomous snakes and poisonous spiders. There is more to fear than guerrillas and vicious animals. Undetected, something lurks under the expansive treetop canopy . . .

Something ancient.

Something dangerous.

Kasai Rex!

 **SEVERED**PRESS

CHECK OUT OTHER GREAT DINOSAUR THRILLERS

SPINOSAURUS
by Hugo Navikov

Brett Russell is a hunter of the rarest game. His targets are cryptids, animals denied by science. But they are well known by those living on the edges of civilization, where monsters attack and devour their animals and children and lay ruin to their shantytowns.

When a shadowy organization sends Brett to the Congo in search of the legendary dinosaur cryptid Kasai Rex, he will face much more than a terrifying monster from the past.

Spinosaurus is a dinosaur thriller packed with intrigue, action and giant prehistoric predators.

LAND OF DEATH
by Eric S Brown & Alex Laybourne

A group of American soldiers, fleeing an organized attack on their base camp in the Middle East, encounter a storm unlike anything they've seen before. When the storm subsides, they wake up to find themselves no longer in the desert and perhaps not even on Earth. The jungle they've been deposited in is a place ruled by prehistoric creatures long extinct. Each day is a struggle to survive as their ammo begins to run low and virtually everything they encounter, in this land they've been hurled into, is a deadly threat.

 SEVEREDPRESS

f facebook.com/severedpress

twitter.com/severedpress

CHECK OUT OTHER GREAT DINOSAUR THRILLERS

WRITTEN IN STONE
by David Rhodes

Charles Dawson is trapped 100 million years in the past. Trying to survive from day to day in a world of dinosaurs he devises a plan to change his fate. As he begins to write messages in the soft mud of a nearby stream, he can only hope they will be found by someone who can stop his time travel. Professor Ron Fontana and Professor Ray Taggit, scientists with opposing views, each discover the fossilized messages. While attempting to save Charles, Professor Fontana, his daughter Lauren and their friend Danny are forced to join Taggit and his group of mercenaries. Taggit does not intend to rescue Charles Dawson, but to force Dawson to travel back in time to gather samples for Taggit's fame and fortune. As the two groups jump through time they find they must work together to make it back alive as this fast-paced thriller climaxes at the very moment the age of dinosaurs is ending.

HARD TIME
by Alex Laybourne

Rookie officer Peter Malone and his heavily armed team are sent on a deadly mission to extract a dangerous criminal from a classified prison world. A Kruger Correctional facility where only the hardest, most vicious criminals are sent to fend for themselves, never to return.

But when the team come face to face with ancient beasts from a lost world, their mission is changed. The new objective: Survive.